● ● ● ● ● ●

The moment Deidra saw that she and Donovan were back, she turned in her seat and watched them as they drew nearer. She looked Donovan up and down and smiled. She didn't have the best grin in the world, but only one of her front teeth was fully missing, which was better than Kyra expected.

"You that boy who used to come over all the time, when y'all was kids," she said to Kyra's husband. "Your name's *Donovan*."

He nodded. He returned her smile half-heartedly.

"Y'all done grew up and got married," Deidra said, her smile brightening.

Donovan couldn't help but express delight at that.

"I knew y'all was gon' get married one day," Deidra continued. "Y'all always said you were *just friends*, but I knew better."

Unlike her husband, Kyra didn't like to see Deidra smile and dote on them, like she'd been a loving mother all these years. There were things that needed to be said. She wasn't willing to play get-along-gang until her dear, old ma answered a few poignant questions.

"Can I talk to you?"

The warm, fuzzy mood vanished when everyone saw Kyra's expression. She was a beautiful woman, with innocent features. The anguish behind her big, brown eyes broke her relatives' hearts.

"Yes, we can talk," Deidra said, pushing herself up from her seat. She looked around the waiting room, which was large, but too small for the talk they needed to have. "You wanna go over…"

"Yeah," Kyra said. She turned and headed for the elevators. "We should go…"

● ● ● ● ● ●

THE REALEST CHRISTMAS EVER

THE REALEST CHRISTMAS EVER

KEITH THOMAS WALKER

KEITHWALKERBOOKS, INC
This is a UMS production

KEITHWALKERBOOKS

Publishing Company
KeithWalkerBooks, Inc.
P.O. Box 331585
Fort Worth, TX 76163

For information write
KeithWalkerBooks, Inc.
P.O. Box 331585
Fort Worth, TX 76163

ISBN-13 DIGIT: 978-0-9967505-0-9
ISBN-10 DIGIT: 0996750509
Library of Congress Control Number: 2015917032
Manufactured in the United States of America

Second Edition

Visit us at www.keithwalkerbooks.com

KEITH THOMAS WALKER

5

This book is for Denise Gary Fizer

MORE BOOKS BY
KEITH THOMAS WALKER

Fixin' Tyrone
How to Kill Your Husband
A Good Dude
Riding the Corporate Ladder
The Finley Sisters' Oath of Romance
Blow by Blow
Jewell and the Dapper Dan
Harlot
Plan C (And More KWB Shorts)
Dripping Chocolate
The Realest Ever
Jackson Memorial
Sleeping With the Strangler
Life After
Blood for Isaiah
Brick House
Brick House 2
One on One

NOVELLAS

Might be Bi (Part One)
Harder
Primal Part One

POETRY COLLECTION

Poor Righteous Poet

FINLEY HIGH SERIES

Prom Night at Finley High
Fast Girls at Finley High

Visit keithwalkerbooks.com for information about these
and upcoming titles from KeithWalkerBooks

ACKNOWLEDGMENTS

Of course I would like to thank God, first and foremost, for giving me the creativity and drive to pursue my dreams and the understanding that I am nothing without Him. I would like to thank my wife for being my first and most important critic, and I would like to thank my mother for always pushing me to be the best I can be. I would like to thank Janae Hampton for being the best advisor, supporter and little sister a brother could ever have. I would also like to thank (in no particular order) Beulah Neveu, Deloris Harper, Denise Fizer, Shelee Stevenson, Melissa Carter, Cathy Atchison, Lanita Irvin, Ramona Weathersbee, Jason Owens, Sharon Blount, BRAB Book Club, and Uncle Steven Thomas, one love. I'd like to thank everyone who purchased and enjoyed one of my books. Everything I do has always been to please you. I know there are folks who mean the world to me that I'm failing to mention. I apologize ahead of time. Rest assured I'm grateful for everything you've done for me!

CHAPTER ONE
PREMATURE

On Monday, December 21st, most of the businesses in Overbrook Meadows were decked out in shimmering reds, greens and silvers. Homes throughout the city were similarly decorated with dazzling light displays that came to life after sunset, filling everyone's heart with Christmas cheer. Even the bah-humbug types couldn't help but admire the season's beauty and enchantment.

By lunchtime that afternoon, Kyra Mitchell had been to nearly every store in Hulen Mall but had yet to find the perfect gift for her husband. This was her third expedition in two days, and she was growing restless as the 25th neared. She would've considered today's trip a bust, but she managed to pick up a few last minute items for other important people in her life. Plus there were still a couple of hours left for her to shop. She dropped her bags off in the car before taking her children Katavia and Quinell to the food court.

While they dined on overpriced gyros that were stuffed to the gills, Kyra picked the little ones' brains, to see if their step-father had mentioned anything to them about what he might like to find under the Christmas tree.

"Get him a football," Katavia, more commonly known as Kat, suggested around a mouthful of grilled beef.

Her mother reached across the table to wipe her face.

"Don't talk with your mouth full," Kyra admonished her.

Kat swallowed and repeated her suggestion. She was a beautiful child; smart and bubbly. Kyra was happy to say that she never had many problems with her daughter. Even her terrible two's were more cute than obnoxious. Kat was going on four now, and she was still a great kid, as far as Kyra was concerned. She knew that her husband felt the same way. He loved Kat and had treated her like his very own since the moment they moved in with him two and a half years ago.

"I don't think he needs another football," Kyra told her.

"He's a coach," Quinell agreed. "He got plenty of footballs at school already."

Kat shrugged and continued with her meal. She began to pick up the meat that fell from her gyro by hand and stuff it into her mouth.

"Use your fork," Kyra reminded her.

Kat followed her mother's instructions, though she tended to hold the utensil like a sword and jab at her food clumsily.

Kyra grinned at her before she asked her son, "What do you think he'd like? Has he said anything?"

Quinell's eyebrows knitted together as he considered that. He shrugged, chuckled and then shook his head.

Kyra narrowed her eyes as she watched him. "What's all that grinning about?"

His smile grew brighter, but he continued to shake his head.

Quinell was tall and thin, a few months shy of his eleventh birthday. He was quiet and fretfully introverted when Kyra packed all of their belongings in a couple of suitcases and fled Arkansas a few years ago. Since then she delighted in watching him blossom like a field of bluebonnets as they settled into their new lives in Texas. She knew her husband was responsible for most of her son's gains.

Not only was Donovan compassionate enough to look past all of Kyra's flaws, but he was uncommonly patient and understanding. He had always been the rock she could hold onto in any storm. Over the past few years, Quinell had come to respect and depend on Donovan as well. Having a stable father in his life had done wonders for the boy's self-esteem.

"I was thinking about what Donovan said he was getting you," Q said, still smiling.

"Oh." That brought a smile to Kyra's face as well. "He talked to you about *my* present?"

"Yeah, but I'm not supposed to tell you."

"Obviously Donovan doesn't know you can't keep a secret," Kyra told him. She leaned forward with her elbows on the table. "What'd he get me?"

"I can keep a secret," Q protested. "That's why I'm not telling you."

"You already told me he told you," Kyra pointed out. "Might as well spill the rest."

"No, Mama, I can't," he insisted. "That's a violation."

"What kind of violation?" she asked with a giggle.

"A man-code violation."

His mother's amusement deepened. *"Man-code? Where'd you get that from, Donovan?"*

The boy nodded. He continued to eat his lunch while she watched him.

"And you didn't point out to Donovan that this *man-code* doesn't apply to you, since you're not a man yet?" his mom teased.

"I'm *almost* a man," he assured her.

Kyra could've contradicted him further, but she found his and Donovan's interactions endearing. As she returned to her own meal, she wondered what her husband had gotten her. If she could figure that out, maybe it would help her decide what to get him in return.

The problem was Donovan had given her so much throughout their lives, she could never keep pace or show her full gratitude. He had been her best friend from grade school through high school, despite the fact that they were from opposite sides of the track. Donovan's family wasn't rich, but he enjoyed a fairytale lifestyle, as far as Kyra was concerned. He had two parents in his home, and their refrigerator was always packed with food, whereas Kyra and her siblings had to depend on one parent who happened to be a drug addict.

Kyra would never forget her lowly school days. Summertime was actually the worst, because there was no free breakfast or lunch provided. As she enjoyed her gyro, she thought back to the time she and her big sister scoured the house for food before eating condiments as a last resort. Most people would scoff at the idea of a ketchup sandwich, but that meal got her through many rough patches.

Fortunately when it came to Kyra, Donovan always shared everything he had. He protected her from schoolyard bullies and provided a safe-haven when school let out for the day. Even if he couldn't offer anything more than a ham sandwich and a juice box, it was always right on time and greatly appreciated.

The best friends were separated for fifteen years when Kyra was forced to move to Arkansas during her 10th grade year, but a friendship as pure as theirs could not be diminished by space, time or even lack of communication.

When she returned to Overbrook Meadows as an adult, Donovan was the only friend she cared to look up. At the time, Kyra was battle-scarred and weary. Donovan quickly resumed his role as her guardian, despite Kyra's insistence that she gain independence. It didn't take long before the couple realized their relationship was deeper than mere friendship. It always had been.

"Fine, keep your little secret," Kyra told her son. "I won't tell you what Donovan got you, either."

His eyes lit up. "Ooh. What'd he get me?"

"Uh-uhn," Kyra laughed. "You gotta wait till Christmas."

"What'd he get me, Mama?" Kat wanted to know.

"I know what he *should've* got you," Kyra said as she rose to her feet, "a box of baby wipes. You're getting filthy over there."

She plucked a handful of napkins from the dispenser as she made her way to the other side of the table. Kat grinned and continued to eat with her free hand while her mother wiped her greasy fingers. When Kyra moved to the other hand, Katavia did too.

"Use your fork," Kyra told her. "You see I'm not getting anywhere, don't you? You're having way too much fun."

The girl continued to eat merrily, and Kyra was distracted by her cellphone ringing. She had to clean her own hands before she retrieved it from her purse. She was not surprised to see her brother's name on the Caller ID. Christmas was right around the corner, and a lot of family members were calling these days with yuletide cheer.

"Hey, what's up?" she said as she returned to her seat.

"I'm at the hospital," Duke said. "Jessica had her baby."

Kyra's face lit up. Her sister wasn't due to deliver for another month, but surprise babies are just as nice.

"Really? That's awesome! When?"

"Just now," Duke said. "But it, it didn't go so good. We almost lost her. We did lose her, for a minute."

The morose quality of his voice shocked Kyra just as much as his words did. Her mouth fell open as a dark chill enveloped her whole body. The brightly lit mall was suddenly shaded by storm clouds. Kyra's mouth was so dry, she could barely respond.

"Wh, what? She almost lost the baby?"

Quinell put his fork down and watched his mother with worried eyes. Even Kat stopped laughing as the mood at the table changed dramatically.

"No," Duke told his sister. "The baby's fine. We almost lost *Jessica*."

Kyra's eyes grew even larger. She never considered her sister would have trouble with this delivery. It was the furthest thought from her mind. Jessica had two children already, and she didn't have a problem delivering either one.

"Wha, what do you mean we almost lost her?"

Kyra's heart was racing. Her eyes filled with tears. She turned away from the table, hoping not to freak her children out any more than she already had.

"She was hemorrhaging," Duke told her. "Lost a lot of blood. They had to, they had to bring her back with a... one of those shock machines."

Kyra brought a fist to her mouth and bit down on her knuckles. She hadn't seen her brother cry since they were children. She couldn't see him now, but she could hear the grief in his voice, the moisture in his nasal passage. Kyra's tears fell as well, and the contents of her stomach threatened to come back up.

This tragedy was unbelievable. Jessica was as healthy as ever the last time Kyra talked to her. No one *dies* during childbirth – not in this country – especially not a few days before Christmas.

Horrible visions filled Kyra's mind. She saw her sister lying pale and lifeless on an operating table while doctors and nurses scrambled to bring her back with a defibrillator. In the background all of the alarms on her monitors were going off because the patient had no vitals. Kyra didn't want to imagine that, but now that it was embedded in her brain, she couldn't shake the thought.

We almost lost her. We did lose her, for a minute.

This didn't seem real. Kyra wanted to curse her brother out for playing such a sick joke, but she knew he wouldn't kid about something like this.

"Can you get here?" Duke asked. "If you can, I think you need to come."

"Is she gonna be alright?" Kyra cried.

"I don't know," Duke said. "She's not even awake right now. They're working on her."

It was an eight hour drive to Little Rock. It didn't sound like Kyra would make it in time, but she told him, "Yes. I'll be there. I'll, I'll come today."

"Alright," Duke said. "Hurry up."

Kyra didn't know how she could hurry to a state so far away, but as she rose to her feet, she tearfully told him, "I will. I promise."

● ● ● ● ● ●

Twenty miles away in the neighborhood of Berry Hill, Donovan lounged with his mother in the kitchen of his childhood home. Beverly called him over that morning to help with more Christmas decorations for her front yard. This time it was an inflatable Santa along with three of his eight reindeer.

Donovan asked his mother to admit that she was engaged in a Christmas war with a neighbor down the street. For every string of lights Mrs. Needham put up, Beverly had to one up her. But she told her son these were coincidences.

"Why would I care what that nosey lady up the road does with her ugly yard?" she asked.

"Is she nosey?" Donovan commented as he knelt to hammer down one of the ties that would keep his mother's bloated Santa from floating away with a strong wind.

"Yes, she is," Beverly confirmed. She shot an evil eye at her neighbor's home. "She can tell you about everybody on this street."

Donovan's mother was thin and short in stature. Her hair was salt and peppery. She wore it short and natural.

She was totally dwarfed by her brawny son, but Beverly never had trouble holding her own. Her mind and body were both quick and spry. She wore wire-rimmed glasses that sat low on her nose at the moment.

"She told Mr. Pete she'd call animal control on me if I keep letting Pearlie in the front yard without her leash," she told her son.

"Really?" Donovan was happy that his mother finally accepted a pet after being widowed for over ten years. He didn't like to hear that one of her neighbors was giving her grief over the leash law.

"She's mad because her son's wife left him for her boss, and he had to move back in with her," Beverly informed him.

"How in the world would you know that?" Donovan asked with a smirk. He looked up and squinted at the sunlight peeping over his mother's shoulder.

"Shirley told me."

Donovan knew Shirley was another neighbor who lived on the next block. She and Beverly had been friends since Donovan was in high school.

"Are you sure Mrs. Needham's the nosey one?" he asked.

"Don't sass me," Beverly told him.

After finishing up her Santa display, Donovan was treated to a nice lunch of tuna sandwiches and key lime pie. Beverly was excited to show him the gifts she bought for Kat, Quinell and Kyra too.

Donovan was pleased to see her aglow with the holiday spirit. It was just three years ago that Kyra returned to Overbrook Meadows and completely changed their lives. Initially Beverly hated the idea that Donovan's childhood crush was back in town. As far as she was concerned, Kyra was and had always been nothing but trouble.

But once Donovan made it clear that he had never loved a woman as much as he loved her, and if he had to pick between her and his mom, Kyra would be the number one woman in his life, Beverly was quick to drop her grievances. She accepted Kat and Q as her grandchildren long before the wedding.

Donovan listened to her rattle on about what seemed like an excessive amount of gifts and then said, "Mama, you can't be spending that much money on them."

"How come I can't?"

"You're retired," he reminded her. "You're on a budget."

"I have room in my budget for Christmas," she assured him. "Plus I got some money put away."

She sat in her favorite loveseat, while her son lounged on the recliner. Donovan's belly was full. The tree in the living room looked beautiful. He treasured the familiar sights and smells of his mother's home. The new addition, Pearlie, was a miniature schnauzer. She sat in Beverly's lap and began to nap as the woman stroked her fur.

"You don't need to dip in your *put away* money for the kids," Donovan advised her. "They'd be happy with a few pairs of socks."

Beverly was aghast to hear such a thing. "*No they would not.* Don't tell me what to spend on my grandbabies."

Donovan had only been married for two and a half years. Hearing her refer to Kyra's children like that put a smile on his face.

"Speaking of grandbabies…" she said.

"Come on, Mama," he said with a roll of his eyes.

"Just tell me if you're working on it."

Although Kat and Q were perfect in every way, Beverly continued to long for a grandchild from her own bloodline; one she could dote on from the moment it was born.

"We're gonna work on that," Donovan promised her.

"When?" Beverly pressed. "You'll be 35 next year. I know Kyra's a year younger, but still..."

"Plenty of people have babies in their mid to late thirties," he informed her.

"Yes, but now is the perfect time. No, the *perfect* time was when you first got married. You both got good jobs. Already got your house..."

Donovan was happy for the distraction when his cellphone rang. Hearing the ringtone he saved for his wife warmed his heart. After two years of marriage he was glad that she still affected him that way.

His expression changed when he answered the phone. By the time he disconnected a couple of minutes later, Donovan was on his feet. His mother rose from her seat as well. She wrung her hands together while she waited to hear what was wrong.

"Kyra's sister is in the hospital," Donovan explained. His big chest rose and fell with his anxious heartbeats. "She had her baby, but it didn't go well. The baby's fine, but they almost lost Jessica. Kyra said they had to bring her back with a defibrillator."

"Oh no." The blood drained from Beverly's face. "Y'all going to Arkansas?"

He nodded. His heart thumped uncomfortably as he made his way to the front door. He prayed the angel of death would pass his family by today. This type of news always came at a bad time, but the holiday season made it feel even worse.

"Wait." Beverly stopped him. "What are you gonna do with the kids? Are you taking them with you?"

Donovan shook his head. He didn't like the idea of taking children to the hospital at times like this. He was sure some of Kyra's relatives in Little Rock could look after them, but wherever he left them might still be a high-stress environment.

"You can leave them with me," Beverly offered. "You and Kyra can travel a lot easier without them."

Donovan's brain was racing. He felt like there were a dozen things he needed to do, but he could only tackle one at a time. He turned and looked into his mother's eyes and forced himself to calm down.

"Alright. That would be great. You don't mind?"

"Of course I don't mind," Beverly said.

She looked as worried as he felt. Donovan was grateful to have her in his life. She was always there for him.

"Come on," she said, taking hold of his hands. "Let's pray."

He lowered his head and closed his eyes as she reached out to God. Her voice was soft, yet confident. The prayer comforted them both. It revealed the depths of Beverly's love for her family. When she finished with, "Amen," Donovan knew that Kyra's sister had a troop of angels fighting for her.

He gave his mother a hug and hurried home to meet up with his wife.

CHAPTER TWO
TRAVELING GRACE

Winter breezes, crystal snowflakes
Cause rosy cheeks to adorn the face
Of her, my love, my heaven sent
Simplistic joy, my unrelenting
Source of warmth. Amazing light
Glows bright from her

Donovan was in Kat's bedroom packing hastily when he heard his family enter the home. He abandoned his task and met them in the front room. As expected, the three of them looked spooked and grief-stricken. Kyra dropped her bags on the couch and stepped to him with wet, anxious eyes. It broke Donovan's heart to see her like that. Her tears always affected him this way, ever since they were children.

Their embrace was powerful and natural. Kyra's world was spinning out of control, but she felt it coming to rest on the proper axis when her husband clutched her tightly. There was no one in her life who could do that for her. Their love was more than resilient. It was destined and spiritual.

"I booked us a flight," he said when they separated. "My mom said she can look after Kat and Quinell while we're gone."

Kyra didn't expect any of that, but she trusted him.

"Our plane leaves in a couple of hours," he continued. "We have to be out of here in thirty minutes, so we'll have time to drop off the kids. I already have your suitcases pulled out."

She nodded. She was so grateful, for everything. She wiped her tears and went to the bedroom to gather her things.

Donovan offered a smile to the children, who were standing there watching quietly. He had plenty to do, but he took a seat on the sofa and beckoned for them to come closer. When they did, he put an arm around both of them.

"How you guys feeling?"

Their eyes gave him the same response. Q was the first to vocalize it.

"Scared."

"That's okay," Donovan told him. "It's okay to be scared. This is a scary time."

"Is Aunt Jessica gonna be okay?" he asked.

"Sure she will," Donovan said. "She's in the hospital. They have everything they need to take care of her."

"We're not going?" he asked. "We have to stay here?"

"It's better that way," Donovan confirmed. "There's a lot going on in Little Rock. I don't want you to be in the hospital all day, around all of those different emotions." He rubbed the top of the boy's head, which was shaved low, like his own. "You'll be alright. Your grandmother has everything ready for Christmas."

"Will you and Mama be home for Christmas?" Quinell asked.

Considering that was four days away, Donovan felt comfortable telling him, "Yeah, we will. And you'll have a great time with Nana while we're gone."

Kat didn't look like she believed that, but she smiled when Donovan gave her a kiss on the cheek.

"I wanna fly in an airplane," Quinell said.

Donovan was happy to see that he wasn't as upset as he was a few minutes ago.

"I couldn't get you a ticket today, but I promise we'll all go on a plane ride one day."

"Me too!" Kat said. "I wanna ride on an airplane."

"I guess I'll let you come too," Donovan said with a grin.

She giggled as he stood and picked her up.

"Now let's get you guys packed, so we can get out of here."

● ● ● ● ● ●

Gathering the children's things wasn't as crucial, because Donovan's mother had a key to his home. They would have to return daily to look after his dogs Doc and Wyatt.

Packing for himself and Kyra was more difficult, given the time restriction. But neither of them had fashion in mind. They focused on the essentials. In the bedroom they moved quickly and efficiently as their time to depart drew nearer.

"I didn't think you'd book a flight," Kyra told him. She was in the bathroom collecting items from the vanity.

"It's a five and a half hour drive," Donovan told her as pulled socks from a dresser drawer. "The flight's only an hour and a half."

"But how can we afford it?" she wondered, "especially around Christmas?"

"My mom's friend got us a hookup on some cancellations. You know the one who's married to a pilot."

"Cheryl?"

Donovan looked back at her and nodded. "Yeah. I'm surprised you remember her."

Kyra offered him a wistful smile as she stepped from the bathroom.

"I'll never forget the way she and your mama were cutting up at our wedding."

Donovan smiled too. Their wedding was such an enchanting event. It was the culmination of a twenty year-long love affair they'd both been denying. Since then, their life together was everything he hoped it would be. Q finally had the stable home and family he'd been thirsting for. And Kat was a continual goofball. Donovan never knew a little girl could be so loving. Every day was a new adventure with young children in the house.

But it was Kyra who completed Donovan the most. She was a voluptuous beauty; soft and doting and fiercely determined. She came to him broken down by life. Now she was focused and determined. She wanted to give Donovan all of the praise for her transformation, but he knew the drive was inside her all along. She just needed to be planted in the right environment, with plenty of love and sunshine.

She sat next to him on the bed, and they subconsciously reached to hold each other's hand.

"Is the baby a boy or a girl?"

Her smile faded. She shook her head. "I don't know. With everything else that was going on, I didn't think to ask."

"But they said the baby's alright?"

She nodded.

"Your sister will be fine, too," he predicted. "I can't wait to talk to her. I haven't seen her since the wedding."

That was the last time Kyra had seen her, too. She was so happy when Jessica and their big brother made the trip from Arkansas.

"You almost ready to go?" Donovan asked.

Kyra's eyes were big and beautiful, her lips pink and full. She didn't have on any makeup, and it was clear that she'd been crying. Even still, she was remarkably attractive.

"Yeah," she said with a sigh. "I know I'll remember something else as soon as we leave. But I can't think of anything I'm missing."

"Toothbrush, deodorant, socks and underwear. That's all a man needs to hit the road."

She grinned. "Well, I'm not a man, and women need a little more than that."

"I guess you can bring a comb," he said. "No one wants to see that kitchen all out of whack."

"I do not have a kitchen." She instinctively reached to the back of her head.

He hugged her tightly. She was momentarily lost in the embrace. She wished she could curl up and stay there forever.

He said, "Of course you don't, sweetie. Your hair miraculously lays down on its own, like no other hair in the history of black women."

She nodded. "Damn right."

● ● ● ● ● ●

The family loaded their gear in Donovan's truck while he went out back to bid farewell to his four-legged buddies. He hated to leave them, especially for days at a time. But his mother was deathly afraid of the beasts. There was no way she'd agree to take them, especially with her miniature schnauzer running around.

Doc was a pitbull and Wyatt was a German shepherd. They were strong and well-fed, but the dogs looked anything but beastly when they interacted with the man of the house. They lived for his attention and his approval.

The weatherman predicted temperatures in the low forties for the next few days, so Donovan didn't worry about leaving them outside in their insulated doghouses. He reentered the home through the backdoor and checked to make sure the lights were off before he locked up and joined his family in the truck.

"Make sure Grandma brings you home *every day* to feed the dogs," he told Q as they backed out of the driveway. "Try to spend some time with them too, if she's not rushing you."

"I will," the boy said. "I love playing with them."

"I wanna play with the dogs!" Kat yelled from the backseat.

"No, I don't want you going back there without Donovan," her mother interjected.

Donovan was confident his dogs would never harm the child, but he didn't contradict Kyra.

"Will y'all be home for Christmas?" Q asked again.

"We will," Kyra said, but she didn't want to promise him something that was out of her control. "We should be."

"If you're not, how will we get our presents?" the boy wondered.

Donovan found it interesting how easily a child's mind could move on to trivial things, even in the midst of a tragedy.

"Santa will deliver your presents wherever you are," he assured him.

"No, for real," Q said.

"Hey, Santa Claus is *magical*," Kyra added, mostly for Kat's benefit. "He can find you, no matter where you are."

"*Santa Claus*!" Kat chimed in.

Quinell was almost past the point of believing in such things, but he didn't want to spoil the mystique for his little sister. He kept his mouth closed, hoping Santa *Mom* and Santa *Dad* would be back by Christmas.

When they arrived at Beverly's house, she was bright and chipper, which helped make Donovan and Kyra's departure seem like no big deal.

"Come on, let's pray," she said in the driveway.

Everyone gathered around and held hands, creating the perfect family unit. Even Katavia quieted down and lowered her gaze.

"Father, we know you're still in the blessing business," Beverly said. "We pray that you lay your hand on Jessica and heal her body, so she can rise up out of that hospital bed and take her baby home. We pray for traveling grace for Donovan and Kyra. Bless the roadways and the air ways. We pray that they get through the airport as smoothly and quickly as possible. In Jesus' name I pray, Amen."

"Amen," they all said.

"Y'all be careful. And kiss that new baby for me," Beverly told Kyra.

"I will," Kyra said with a smile. "Thank you so much, Miss Beverly."

The women embraced. Donovan watched them before stepping closer to hug them both. He kissed his mother on the cheek and knelt to hug and kiss his children. Kyra did the same.

After everyone said their goodbyes, the couple hit the road. Worry replaced their smiles before they made it to the freeway. Neither of them wanted to believe that women still died in childbirth. If things like that did happen, it couldn't possibly happen to someone they knew. Not today.

Not at Christmastime.

CHAPTER THREE
CRACK MAMA

I am the darkened alleyway
Where addicts writhe and demons prey
The gutter with the filthy stench
The body crumpled on the bench
I am the cruel and vicious thing
That forms nightmares from blissful dreams
The beast that lurks on darkened floors
The sound behind the basement door

Kyra called her brother as Donovan drove them to the airport.

"Hey. You gonna be able to make it?"

"We're on our way to the airport," she told him. "How's Jessica doing?"

"She hasn't woke up yet," Duke informed her.

Kyra's heart quivered. "What do you mean? Is she in a coma?"

"Yeah. But it's medically-induced. They moved her from labor and delivery to ICU. They're giving her blood; putting back what she lost during the delivery."

"How much blood did she lose?"

"I forgot what they said." Duke sounded stressed and exhausted. "She went into labor at six this morning."

"She called and told me she was headed to the hospital," Kyra told him. "But she thought they were gonna send her home. I was getting worried, and then I got the call from you."

"I knew something was wrong when it was taking so long," Duke said. "She never had labor problems before. Gary was in there with her the whole time. He came out, looking as white as a ghost. He said she was bleeding bad, and the doctors had to work on her. They made him leave. I never seen him so shook."

Kyra had never met her sister's current boyfriend, but she heard Gary was a good man. He proposed to Jessica a few weeks ago.

"Who else is at the hospital with you?"

Duke rattled off the names of his wife and a few cousins and friends of the family.

"When they give her the blood, she'll come around?" Kyra asked.

"That's what they're saying. But they won't try to wake her up until they think she's strong enough."

The tears spilled from Kyra's eyes again. Her big sister had always been feisty and resilient. She didn't want to see her in ICU, with a multitude of tubes and monitors attached to her. But that wasn't the only reason Kyra dreaded returning to Arkansas.

"Alright, I'll call you when we land."

"What about the baby?" Donovan asked before she ended the call.

"Oh, what about the baby?" she asked her brother.

"Fat and healthy," Duke said. "Seven pounds, two ounces. Twenty-two inches long. That baby ain't got no problems."

Kyra smiled pensively. "A boy or a girl?"

Jessica had plenty of prenatal visits, but she chose to keep the sex of the baby a surprise this time.

"It's a boy."

"Did they name him yet?"

"Yep," Duke said. "Gary Junior." He chuckled.

"Alright, I'll call you when we get to Little Rock," Kyra said.

"Okay, baby Sis. Be safe."

Kyra disconnected and relayed all of the new information to Donovan. He was contemplative as he drove and listened. His memories of Kyra's older sister were mostly shaded with sympathy, because of their family's upbringing.

When they first met, Donovan and Kyra were in the fourth and third grade respectively. His mother once told him Kyra had a pound puppy disposition that compelled Donovan to befriend her. But he never saw it like that. As far as he was concerned, they were just two kids who happened to be in search of a playmate that day.

As their friendship deepened, it became obvious that Kyra's home life left much to be desired. Donovan was young and naïve, but he was old enough to know that some people were less fortunate than others. Thankfully, his mother had always taught him to share. Initially Kyra rebuffed his offers, but over time she came to appreciate his giving nature.

Kyra's mother, Deidra, was a crack addict. The unpredictable and occasionally dangerous conditions at home led Kyra to spend as much time with Donovan as possible as they transitioned from childhood to adolescence. Kyra's siblings didn't have such an outlet, and they were left to fend for themselves.

By the time Duke made it to high school, he was skipping school and doing time in juvenile detention centers. Jessica didn't get into much trouble, but the things she'd seen at home hardened her over time. Initially Donovan found her to be bitter and uncaring. He often complained that she didn't do enough to help Kyra. But he came to understand that Jessica was a victim herself, and there was only so much help she could offer.

For his part, Donovan couldn't do much either, but he always tried to make his friend's life a little better; a little less stressful. Sometimes his interference got him in trouble, like the time he called the police to report a drug dealer who had opened up shop in Kyra's home. And they would never forget the time he attacked her mother's boyfriend. Donovan was only sixteen at the time, but he didn't hesitate when Kyra told him the pervert had made a move on her.

The perilous existence Deidra created for her children came to an end when she was arrested for forgery during Kyra's sophomore year at Finley High. It was her fourth conviction, so she was sent to prison. Her children had to go live with relatives in Little Rock. Donovan was devastated when Kyra tearfully delivered the news. Tears leaked from his own eyes later that day when he begged his mother to take Kyra in, so she could remain in Overbrook Meadows and hopefully avoid the fate that awaited her in Arkansas.

Beverly was against the idea, but Donovan and Kyra had maintained a platonic relationship since grade school. It was a shock to everyone, especially her son, when Beverly agreed to take in the needy child. Of all of Donovan's high school memories, he would have to say the time Kyra became a member of their family was the best. Unfortunately it only lasted five months.

One afternoon, much like with Adam and Eve, Donovan began to notice Kyra's soft lips and the small bulges of her nipples beneath her tee-shirt. Neither of them could say who initiated their first kiss, but it only took one time to ruin everything. Beverly stepped in and caught them groping and dry-humping, like the horny teenagers they were. And that was all she wrote. She booked Kyra a flight to Little Rock the very next day.

Because of their transgression, Donovan didn't see his best friend for a decade and a half. He now knew what had become of her and her siblings in Arkansas. Fortunately all three of them managed to avoid the statistics and build decent lives for themselves. Duke worked as a big rig mechanic. He was married with three kids, and Jessica just delivered her third child.

"How long has Jessica been with Gary?" Donovan asked as he drove.

"About three years now," Kyra told him. "I hear he's a good dude."

"What does he do for a living?"

"He sells cars," Kyra told him, "at a Jeep dealership."

"That's a good job. One of my friends sells Hondas. He gets to drive whatever he wants."

"Yeah," Kyra mused. "Jessica's always rolling in something new."

"Was he at our wedding?"

"No. They were going out when we got married, but he couldn't make it."

"So you've never met him?"

She shook her head.

"Is this the first child they have together?" Donovan asked.

"No. They have Damiqua. She's one and a half."

Donovan's eyebrows rose.

Kyra smirked. "You think that's a ghetto name?" she guessed.

"No, it's... unique," he stated.

"So it would be fine for our daughter?"

"No," he said right away. "Not because it's ghetto. But we can't have *two* Damiqua's in the family."

She chuckled softly. They talked about having a child one day but hadn't made any serious efforts other than Donovan asking Kyra to get off the pill.

"Who else is at the hospital?" he wondered. "Anyone I should be prepared for?"

"I'm the one who needs to be prepared," Kyra said. Her smile faltered.

"Why is that?" her husband asked. "Do you expect to see some unfriendly faces?"

She shrugged and looked out of the passenger window. "I don't know about *unfriendly*, but everyone I see will bring a bunch of bad memories." An uncomfortable shiver rolled down her body.

Donovan reached and took hold of her hand. Kyra turned and looked at him. She smiled softly as he gave her hand a comforting squeeze.

When Kyra moved to Arkansas at the age of sixteen, she lived with her Aunt Joyce, who was already burdened with five children in a low-income neighborhood. After graduating high school, Kyra's choice of suitors was typical for girls in that area. Quinell's father was a low-level dealer. He was stabbed to death by another one of his girlfriends. Katavia's father was a heroin addict. He was currently serving life in prison after a run-of-the-mill burglary turned into a home invasion murder.

Donovan wished he could say his wife was a shining beacon in what she described as a dark, scary time, but that wasn't the case. Kyra was once addicted to drugs herself. CPS got involved, and she lost custody of Kat and Quinell for a few months. When she got them back, Kyra fled Little Rock and reunited with her best friend in Overbrook Meadows. She hadn't been back since. Today she had to return to her field of nightmares to look after her sister and face her demons.

But things were different now. She was married, and Donovan would be by her side the whole time. Kyra felt the strength and love in his touch as he caressed her hand.

Even still, her eyes filled with tears as she contemplated the misery that may be awaiting them in Arkansas.

"Everything will be fine," Donovan assured her.

Kyra nodded, and she was able to keep her tears in for now.

CHAPTER FOUR
LITTLE ROCK INTERNATIONAL

When they arrived at the airport, Kyra found the experience to be fast-paced and nerve-racking. She was sure she wouldn't have made it without Donovan, who had been on dozens of flights during his college football days. He knew where to park, how to get their boarding passes printed and where to check in.

Kyra held onto his hand as he led her through the airport, which was crowded with Christmas travelers. He was in a hurry, but he slowed whenever the sights and sounds of the terminal became a distraction for his wife.

When they reached their gate, he hugged her from behind while they stood in line for boarding. Kyra felt like the luckiest girl in the world whenever his strong arms were wrapped around her. She loved that he was always affectionate, regardless of their surroundings. Some of the ladies she worked with complained that their husbands never held their hands or kissed them in public.

"When was the last time you were on a plane?" Donovan asked over her shoulder.

Kyra shook her head as her mind was filled with unpleasant memories. "Are you serious?"

"Sorry." He grinned sheepishly. "I forgot."

"You forgot that your mom dragged me out of your house and threw me on a plane?" she asked. She turned towards him, and he was happy to see that she was smiling.

"I think my brain may have blocked it out," he offered.

"I wish I could say the same. I had nightmares about that day for years."

"I'm sorry." He leaned down and kissed her.

"It's not your fault," she said.

He kissed her again, softer this time. His affection caused a slow burn to build in Kyra's chest. She felt a tingle in all of her extremities.

"She wouldn't have done that if you didn't seduce me," Donovan joked.

Her eyes widened. "You're blaming *me* for that kiss?"

"I was a good boy," he said. "Everybody knows that."

"Oh, and I was a bad girl?"

"Well, you were from the hood," he reminded her. "And you had that tight tee-shirt on that day. And then you turned the air down real low, knowing what would happen."

She couldn't help but laugh at that. "You know I never touched Miss Beverly's thermostat! She would've killed me."

She thought back to that fateful day twenty years ago. When she was in Little Rock, the memory of their first kiss broke her heart time after time. But now that she had returned to Overbrook Meadows and kissed Donovan a few more times, and made love to him, and married the man of her dreams, Kyra could see the humor in their first bumbling attempt at love.

"You probably turned the air down yourself, because you wanted to see what you saw," she told him.

"I never touched Mama's thermostat, either," he laughed.

"Then maybe they perked up on their own."

"What did?"

"What were you talking about?"

"We're talking about the same thing," he assured her. "I just want to hear you say it."

"What?" She lowered her voice. "My *nipples*?"

He grinned devilishly and nodded. "Best ones I've ever seen."

"You mean when you were seventeen?"

"Yeah and since then."

Kyra's face heated. She giggled. "I'm glad you like them."

• • • • • •

When they boarded their plane, Donovan noticed his wife was anxious as they took their seats. Her anxiety increased when the flight crew completed their safety demonstration and the plane began to taxi down the runway. He took hold of her hand again, but it wasn't enough. Kyra let go of him and gripped his thigh instead. When the plane lifted from the ground, her nails dug into him so hard he had to clench his jaws shut to avoid shouting.

"*Hey...*" He rubbed the top of her hand but didn't try to remove her talons from his flesh. "You okay?"

Kyra looked his way with wide, frightful eyes. She shook her head tersely. She looked past him and stared at the rapidly shrinking landscape beyond his window. She squeezed her eyes closed and began to take short, quick breaths.

"You've flown before," he reminded her.

"One, one time," she told him.

"One time?"

"The time your mom sent me away."

Donovan watched her with wonderment. When it came to street smarts, Kyra had more experience, hands down. She could take five dollars to the grocery store and come back with a full Sunday dinner. But when it came to average American experiences, Kyra was far behind him. He found that adorable. He loved to experience new things with her, even if they weren't new to him.

He put an arm around her and pulled her closer. She was stiff at first, but after a few moments she leaned into him.

He rested his head on hers and said, "Planes don't crash anymore."

"What about 9-11?"

"You should never say that on a plane," he whispered. "But if someone does try to hijack us with a box cutter, I promise to take him out."

Kyra grinned. She fully believed that. She knew Donovan would stand up to a grizzly bear to protect his family.

"What about the plane that crashed in the Hudson River?"

"That pilot *landed* in the Hudson River," he said. "He's a hero, and no one was killed."

"What about Harrison Ford?" she asked. "He crashes planes all the time."

Donovan chuckled, wondering if she would ask about the Hindenburg next.

"It's not funny," Kyra said and eased the death grip on his leg. She opened her eyes and saw that they were among the clouds now. The view was frightening, but also very beautiful.

She looked around and noticed how cramped her husband was. His knees were touching the seat in front of him, even though the passenger in that seat wasn't leaning back.

"Now *that's* funny," she said.

"What's that?"

"The way they got my big, strong man squeezed up in here."

"I'm glad you find it amusing," he said and shifted his bulk in the small chair. "Coach seats aren't made for fat people or tall people."

Donovan wasn't fat at all, but at six feet, four inches, he was plenty tall. Plus he was nearly as muscular as he had been during his college football days. It suddenly occurred to Kyra how much he had given of himself that day. In addition to the uncomfortable plane seats, he had changed all of his holiday plans at the drop of a hat and made arrangements for their trip to Little Rock. Kyra didn't have to do anything but follow his lead. He was the only person in her life that she could fully depend on.

"Thank you," she told him.

His eyes narrowed in confusion. "For what?"

"For booking this flight. For everything."

His expression didn't change. "I don't know what you mean. We had to go to Little Rock. I care about your family. What did you think I would do?"

Kyra's heart swelled with love. He was genuinely unaware of how amazing he was. Given the bad choices she'd made in life, she didn't feel that she deserved a man like him. Donovan had been overlooking her faults since the third grade. He loved her unconditionally. Loving him back didn't seem like an adequate form of repayment. It wasn't nearly enough.

● ● ● ● ● ●

Kyra was on her phone again the moment their plane touched down in Little Rock. There were a lot of her relatives at the hospital, but her brother was her go-to source for information.

"Yo," Duke said. "Where you at?"

"Plane just landed," Kyra reported. Her chest was tight with dread again. "We haven't gotten off yet. How's she doing?"

"No change yet. They don't wanna try to wake her up until they think she's strong enough to handle it."

"She's gonna be alright?"

Kyra knew her brother had no way of knowing the answer to that, but she needed him to say yes. She remained in her seat while the other passengers began to stand and retrieve their carry-on items from the overhead storage. Donovan didn't budge either.

"Jessica's a fighter," Duke replied. "You know she's too strong to go out like that."

Kyra thought his assurance would make her feel better, but it didn't. Her empty stomach continued to twist in knots.

"Do you need a ride from the airport?" Duke asked. "Me and Melvin are about to go get something to eat. I can pick you up."

Melvin was her nephew; Duke's his oldest son. "Hold on," she told him and then asked her husband, "Do we need my brother to pick us up?"

Donovan shook his head. "No. I got a car reserved."

Kyra's eyes brightened. She told Duke, "No. We have a rental."

"Alright," he said. "We should be back by the time y'all get here."

When she got off the phone, Kyra asked Donovan, "When did you get a rental car?"

"Before you got home. Right after I booked the flight."

She knew her husband had everything under control, but his thoroughness continued to amaze her. "Thank you."

"Don't thank me for stuff like that. You can thank me for buying flowers on our anniversary – but not for being there for you in an emergency."

She nodded and her eyes filled with tears again. Donovan assumed it was because of her sister's predicament, and it was, for the most part. But Kyra was so grateful for their marriage that at times it was hard to keep her emotions in check.

When the last passenger passed them, Donovan squeezed out of his seat and made it to a standing position. He reached and helped his wife up before stretching his travel-weary legs.

• • • • • •

Donovan called his mother as they headed to the baggage claim. He asked if she could make a reservation for them at a Motel 6 near the hospital.

When he returned his phone to his pocket, Kyra told him, "You didn't have to do that. We can stay with Aunt Joyce or one of my cousins."

"I don't want to inconvenience anyone," he told her. "I hate sleeping on couches. And I can't ask anyone to give up their bedroom."

She didn't argue.

They gathered their luggage and picked up an SUV from Enterprise. When they left the airport, Kyra's tension continued to surge as she directed Donovan to the hospital. She didn't think she'd be able to hold it together if they got there and learned Jessica had taken a turn for the worst. Christmas would never be the same if she lost her big sister.

Kyra realized she didn't feel excited about her new nephew. Gushing over the latest addition to their family would have to wait until the doctors upgraded Jessica's condition and brought her out of her coma.

When they made it to the hospital, Kyra's apprehension got the best of her when Donovan couldn't find a parking spot. They ascended floor after floor in the main parking garage, but every spot was taken.

"We should've used the valet," she complained. "We're not gonna find anything in here. We'll have to go all the way back down."

"Calm down," Donovan said, noticing her stress. He reached and placed a hand on her knee, hoping to stop it from bouncing. "Look, there's a spot right there."

Kyra followed his gaze and saw that they were approaching an empty space. She placed her hand over his. "I'm sorry. I'm trying to stay calm."

"It's okay," he said. "I understand."

Donovan parked the rental, and they hurried to the elevator. When they got to the ground floor, they rushed from the garage and into the hospital. They didn't have to stop at the information desk, because Duke had already told them what floor and room to find them in. They took the elevator up to an ICU unit and were greeted by several familiar faces in the waiting room.

Kyra's aunt Joyce was there with her sons. She didn't see her brother, but his wife Sheryl was there with their youngest daughter Tara. Everyone was eager to greet Kyra and her husband, but she didn't have a smile for any of them. She barely heard what they were saying as they clamored around her.

"Where's Duke?" she asked his wife.

"He's with her now," Sheryl said. "Come on, I'll take you to her room. They'll only let four or five of us back there at a time."

She grabbed Kyra's hand, and Kyra reached back and found Donovan's. They followed Sheryl through a set of double doors, and the scenery changed drastically. The floor changed from carpeted to tiled. The unit had the unmistakable scent of sanitizers and medicine. There was also an underlying aroma of sickness and death. All around them nurses and techs were busy with the important task of saving lives.

Sheryl led them past several rooms that were occupied with patients in varying stages of distress. Some were intubated, while others sat up in bed and conversed with their relatives. They stopped at room 408, and finally Kyra laid eyes upon her sister. There were other people in the room, but Kyra only saw Jessica.

Her big sister didn't look big at all as she lay motionless under the hospital sheets with IV lines providing blood and other fluids. Kyra knew she had only been there since this morning, but Jessica looked like she'd been in this state for days, months even. Kyra's hand slipped away from Donovan's as she approached the bed. She didn't notice her relatives step aside to make way for her. Donovan followed close enough to support her, if the sight proved too much for his wife and she became weak.

Tears spilled from Kyra's eyes as she reached and took hold of her sister's hand. It felt limp and lifeless, but Jessica's hand wasn't cold, so Kyra knew her blood continued to flow. She reached with her other hand and touched her sister's face. Jessica's eye sockets were dark, her cheeks slightly sunken. She had brown skin that looked ashen and void of the exuberance Kyra was used to seeing. She brushed the hair away from Jessica's forehead and then ran her fingers across her dry lips.

"What are you trying to do?" she asked her. "It's Christmastime. You need to be up and out of this bed." She sniffled and brushed the tears off her cheek with her shoulder. "You got a new baby who needs you. You gotta get better and get out of here."

Kyra's words became unintelligible as her crying worsened. Her family gradually left the room and allowed her the private moment – everyone except Donovan. Kyra felt his presence as he stepped forward and stood beside her. He put an arm around her, and she turned and cried on his shoulder.

When they left her sister's room, Kyra and Donovan made their way to the nurse's station and found Jessica's RN.

"She's doing a lot better," the nurse told them. "She had a big scare during her delivery, but she's been stable since they brought her up from L&D. I talked to her doctor a couple of hours ago. He's in the hospital, if you need me to page him for you. He said Jessica's a lot stronger, and she should be awake tonight or tomorrow morning."

Kyra didn't like that timetable, but she had to accept it. She and Donovan returned to the waiting room, and her family rushed to greet her again. This time Kyra took the time to hug everyone. Her relatives managed to put a smile on her face.

Duke was there with his wife and all three of their children. Aunt Joyce was accompanied by Kyra's twin cousins Tevin and Kevin. Uncle Billy had come too, along with Uncle Harold and Aunt Rachel. Kyra didn't recognize a few of the grinning faces. Aunt Joyce introduced one of them as her boyfriend William. And Kyra met Jessica's boyfriend Gary for the first time. He was a handsome man, though today's troubles were clearly wearing him down.

Kyra looked around and realized her relatives had monopolized nearly the whole waiting room.

"We might as well have a family reunion up in here," Uncle Billy said, and they all laughed.

When things settled down, Donovan asked his wife, "Are you hungry?"

Kyra didn't think she was, but she hadn't eaten anything since lunchtime. It was now a couple of hours past sunset. Her stomach grumbled at the thought of food. They went to the cafeteria and brought back cold sandwiches and chips.

After dinner they took a trip to the nursery to see Jessica's baby boy. Gary Jr. was adorable. He was sleeping, so Kyra declined the nurse's offer to hold him. But she and Donovan watched and smiled at him for a while. He seemed totally perfect, surely not capable of causing any harm, but his birth had almost ended it all for his mother.

"You're lucky you're so cute," Kyra told the infant. She smiled lovingly, and all was forgiven.

When they made it back to the waiting room, Kyra had to admit that it was nice to spend time with her family, especially so close to Christmas. She returned to her sister's room and sat with her for a couple of hours, hoping Jessica would wake up on her own.

Around midnight Donovan came to the room and roused his wife. Kyra didn't realize she had fallen asleep in the bedside chair. She returned to the waiting room with him and found that most of the visitors had gone home for the night. That was fine, because it left the biggest couch in the room vacant.

Donovan and Kyra took a seat and reclined on the comfy sofa. He never asked if she wanted to leave the hospital and return in the morning. Within minutes she had fallen asleep again in his protective embrace. Donovan gave in to his body's demand for rest shortly afterwards.

CHAPTER FIVE
SMALL WORLD

The next morning Donovan awakened feeling stiff and exhausted. The first thing he became aware of was his wife leaning heavily against him, and a slight smile curved his lips. He looked around and saw that the waiting room was sparsely populated with Kyra's relatives and a few members from another family.

There were no sun rays squeezing through the window blinds, but he could see that the sun was on the rise. He checked his watch and confirmed it was almost seven a.m.

His brief movement caused Kyra to stir. She snuggled against him reflexively and then opened her eyes and looked into his.

"You didn't sleep well," she noticed.

"I slept fine. How about you?"

"As good as to be expected," she replied.

"The doctor's coming this morning?"

"Yeah. He's supposed to wake her, if she's not up already."

"Is it too early to go check?"

She yawned. "What time is it?"

"Almost seven."

"I don't think it's too early," she said and sat up on the sofa. Her body felt achy in a few spots, but overall she was well-rested. She knew that was because her hubby made the perfect pillow.

Donovan stood and stretched and said, "You ready?"

Kyra nodded, and he helped her to her feet.

● ● ● ● ● ●

The nurse told them the doctor would be in at nine. Until then they were allowed to visit with Jessica. They entered her room and saw that Duke and his wife Sheryl were there already. She had her nose in a book, while he fiddled with his cellphone.

"Morning," Donovan told them as he and Kyra approached Jessica's bed.

Duke and his wife returned the greeting.

Kyra thought her sister looked a lot better today. Her face had a lot more color. Someone had brushed her hair back in a ponytail. Her mane was dark and healthy. Kyra reached and held her hand. She smiled down at her sister. Jessica even felt warmer than she did yesterday.

"You gon' wake up today," Kyra told her.

"Yeah, she is," Duke agreed. He rose from his seat and stood beside her. "She's doing a lot better. I see her eyes fluttering sometimes, like she's trying to wake up. But the nurse says she can't right now, because of the meds the doctor got her on. They're already starting to wean her off, though. She might be woke before the doctor gets here."

"I hope so," Kyra said.

"Have y'all seen the baby yet?" her brother asked.

"Yeah, but it was late. I didn't hold him. Didn't want to wake him up."

"So you didn't feel how heavy he is..." Duke said.

Kyra shook her head. She smiled at the thought of her precious nephew. "We might go see him again, before the doctor gets here."

"How about you?" Duke asked Donovan. "How you holding up?"

"I'm good," he said.

Kyra studied her husband's features and saw that his eyes were a lot quicker than they were a few minutes ago. It felt great to have her brother standing on one side of her with her husband on the other. She didn't realize how much she missed her family.

"Who did her hair?" she asked Duke.

"Sheryl did."

Kyra looked back and gave her a thankful smile.

"We were about to go see what they have for breakfast," Duke told them. "Y'all wanna go?"

Kyra looked her husband's way.

He nodded. "Coffee would be nice."

● ● ● ● ● ●

Donovan got his coffee as well as two biscuits smothered in gravy with three sausage patties crumbled on top. They enjoyed breakfast with Duke and his wife. Afterwards the group went to the nursery to see little Gary. They weren't surprised to find Gary *Sr.* there. Kyra was happy that Jessica had finally found a good man, after a history of dating thugs and losers.

Little Gary was fussy that morning, but no one minded. They all took a shot at being the one who could quiet him down – everyone except Donovan, that is.

"Girl, I'd break that little thing," he said when Kyra tried to hand him over.

"Might as well give it a shot," Duke encouraged him. "What you gon' do when you and Kyra pop one out?"

Donovan chuckled at that and continued to shake his head.

Kyra found his reluctance amusing.

When they returned to Jessica's unit, she was delighted to see a woman she knew in the waiting room. It was Felisha, her sister's best friend. Kyra was not happy to see another woman she recognized standing at Felisha's side. Her name was Mary.

"Wow, *Kyra*! Girl, it's good to see you!"

Felisha came forward, and the women embraced.

"You too!" Kyra said. "How have you been? It's been too long!"

"I know," Felisha agreed. "You *know* you need to come home more often."

"I know."

The women separated and watched each other with warm smiles.

"Have you seen Jessica yet?" Kyra asked.

"Yeah," Felisha said. "But they made us leave when the doctor came to check on her."

"Her doctor's here?" Kyra asked, her eyes widening. "I wanna talk to him. He's supposed to wake Jessica up today."

Felisha nodded. "She was already waking up, but they said we had to leave for a second."

Kyra's heart began to kick harder. A humongous wave of relief crashed over her. *"Jessica's waking up?"* She turned, heading for her sister's room, but Felisha stopped her.

"Wait. They told us to step out for a second," she reminded her. "They said they'd come get us when the doctor was ready."

Kyra calmed herself. Her grin was wide and anxious. Jessica was waking up! She couldn't wait to get in there and see her.

She looked over at the woman who accompanied Felisha, and her smile faded. Mary was staring at her with barely concealed malice. The woman had fair skin and dark, shoulder-length hair. She didn't have on any makeup today, but Kyra knew that she liked to wear bright red lipstick that made her look easy and available – in her opinion.

But Kyra's opinion was biased. Mary was part of a dark past that made her blood run cold whenever she had to confront it. Oftentimes the memories condemned her so thoroughly, she couldn't stop a flow of tears from springing from her eyes. Kyra hoped that wouldn't happen today, but being this close to her old life affected her on a physical level.

"How you doing?" she said, hoping they could speak and go on about their business. Kyra's face was deadpan, her eyes uninviting.

"I'm fine," Mary said. "You know Leonard got *life*, don't you?"

The comment was like a slap to the face. Kyra was sure that was Mary's intent, and she was determined not to react. Only a slight twitch of her eye revealed her inner turmoil.

Donovan didn't have a visible reaction either, but he quickly became defensive of Kyra and wary of Mary. Leonard was Katavia's father. He was a gang-banger-turned-heroin addict. The state of Arkansas had deemed him a murderer as well. Donovan was against the mass incarceration of black men, but Leonard was one brother who deserved to be in prison. Good riddance.

"I'm sorry to hear that," Kyra said tersely, in response to Mary's question.

The woman looked her up and down. She checked out Donovan and the rest of their crew before continuing, "Everybody think he fell off the deep end because of what *you* did."

Everyone had something to say then, starting with Kyra's big brother.

"Yo, what the hell?"

Donovan almost took a step forward, but he stilled himself. He was a powerful man, and Mary was a petite woman. Even Kyra had twenty pounds on her. He knew his wife could handle this, but he was there for her, just in case.

"Don't put that on me," Kyra snapped. "I didn't have nothing to do with that."

"Wait, hold on," Felisha said, stepping between the women. "This ain't the time or place," she told Mary. Her expression was disapproving.

"Whatever." Mary blew them off and headed for the elevator.

"Kyra, I'm sorry for that," Felisha said before she followed her.

As the women left the unit, Kyra's friends and family came forward to offer support.

Even Sheryl, Duke's soft-spoken wife, agreed, "She was completely out of line."

They felt bad for Donovan, too.

"She wrong for bringing that man up around you," Duke told him.

"I'm not tripping on that," Donovan assured them. "She felt like she had something to say, and she said it. It's over now."

"Why was she here?" Kyra asked her aunt Joyce. "Is she friends with Jessica?"

"Felisha's friends with Jessica, and Mary's friends with Felisha," Joyce explained. "All three of them hang out sometimes. They all friends."

Kyra didn't recall Jessica ever hanging out with Leonard's sister, but she had been gone for three years. A lot could happen in that time.

When Donovan was afforded a moment alone with his wife, he saw that Kyra was more shaken up than she let on.

"What's that girl's problem?" he asked. "She's blaming you for Leonard going to prison?"

Kyra nodded. Her brow was furrowed in anger. "Jessica told me that a little while ago," she revealed.

"But why?" Donovan asked.

"They said he was trying to get clean. But when he came to Overbrook Meadows to get me and Katavia back, he couldn't take it when I wouldn't go. But that's a lie. They're making excuses for why he turned out like he did."

As a Christian, Donovan didn't like to keep anger in his heart. But he struggled to forgive his wife's ex-boyfriend. He held Leonard responsible for Kyra experimenting with drugs. She might have taken them of her own free will, but it was Leonard who had supplied the poison.

"You didn't have anything to do with him breaking into people's houses," Donovan assured his wife. "I know you're not buying into that. He killed a man so he could get high. That was *his* choice."

"I know." Kyra shook her head. Her expression was pained. "But it reminds me of what I did to my kids. I hate thinking about it."

Her eyes glistened. Donovan felt her pain. He knew that she considered Q and Kat's brief stint with CPS a tremendous failure on her part. He wrapped his arms around her. Kyra welcomed the support.

"Your past is important," he told her. "It's a part of who you are."

She nodded and pressed her face into his chest. If she cried, she didn't want anyone to see.

"But your future's a lot more important," Donovan continued. "*Our* future is."

She looked up at him and managed a weak smile. Her bad deeds in Little Rock were definitely behind her. She and Donovan had the rest of their lives to build on the strides she'd made since returning to Texas and reuniting with him.

A commotion near the entrance of the unit caught their attention. Kyra's family clamored around a doctor who appeared to have good news, judging by the smile on his face.

Kyra and Donovan headed that way, and joy quickly replaced their sour moods.

"She is awake," the doctor was saying. He wore a full beard and turban. His accent was thick. "She doesn't have all of her strength back, but she's ready and eager to see all of you."

The family expressed relief and happiness. They all tried to squeeze by the doctor, but a nurse standing behind him said, "Wait. *Five at a time.* Y'all know that."

After a brief debate, Kyra, Duke, Aunt Joyce, Uncle Harold and Melvin got to go first. When they entered Jessica's room, they saw that Gary Sr. was already there with the baby. Technically that put them over the visitor limit, but if the nurse noticed, she didn't complain.

Kyra cried tears of joy when she threw her arms around her sister and hugged her tightly.

"Don't you ever scare us like that again!"

Jessica was excited and confused to see her little sister in Arkansas. "When'd you get here?"

Her voice was soft and raspy and a little drugged, but Kyra was ecstatic to hear her speaking.

"Yesterday," she said. "Me and Donovan flew in."

"Really? It's good to see you," Jessica replied. "But I'm alright. I didn't mean to scare y'all."

Kyra wondered if her sister knew that she had no heartbeat for twenty scary seconds after her delivery. Surely the doctor had told her.

"Girl, you know I had to come make sure you were okay," she said. "Plus I had to see my nephew too! Your baby is so *precious*. Makes me wish I had another one."

Jessica smiled at that. She looked over at Gary, who sat with the infant in his arms. She didn't have the strength to hold her baby yet, but the look in her eyes made it clear that was her first priority.

After visiting for twenty minutes, Duke backed away from the bed and told her, "We're gonna let some of the other folks out there come see you. They'll only let five of us in at a time."

"Who else is out there?" Jessica asked.

"Who *ain't* out there is a better question," Duke said. He chuckled. "You are loved, Jessie. You never have to wonder about that."

Jessica smiled warmly. Duke was the only person in her life who still called her *Jessie*. Their mother gave her the nickname, but she hadn't been around for nearly twenty years.

When they returned to the waiting room, Kyra's heart was racing. Her smile was ear to ear. She sought her husband in the crowd. She was eager to update him on her sister's condition.

She spotted Donovan and headed his way, but two new visitors stepped off the elevator and completely stole her attention. They were both relatives, but Kyra knew this reunion would not be pleasant. The sight of them opened old, jagged wounds, much like running into Leonard's sister had done.

Kyra hadn't seen Aunt Ruth in over two years, though they lived in the same city. Ruth offered her a safe haven when Kyra fled Little Rock, but her place of refuge quickly turned into a nightmare. It hadn't taken long to realize Ruth was a deceitful, spiteful woman. Her only goal was to use Kyra and her children for financial gain.

Even more shocking was the woman Ruth brought with her. Kyra almost didn't recognize her, but Deidra had strong features that hadn't changed much in two decades.

Plus no one can forget what their own mother looks like.

Kyra was so befuddled, she nearly fainted.

Donovan spotted Aunt Ruth, and he recognized Kyra's mother, too. He couldn't believe that after a lifetime of drugs and debauchery, Deidra had chosen this moment to rise from the land of the lost. His defenses were on high alert as he swiftly made his way across the waiting room and stood at his wife's side.

CHAPTER SIX
MAMA

"Damn, Kyra," Aunt Ruth said. "You come all the way to Little Rock and didn't tell nobody. We could've rode with you."

Kyra couldn't find her voice. Her mouth hung open. Her eyes were locked on her mother's. Everyone was watching Deidra. The woman was of medium height, about thirty pounds overweight. She wore black slacks with a blouse that was pretty but outdated. Her winter coat was oversized.

Kyra hadn't lived with her mother since her sophomore year of high school. Deidra went to prison for four years, and her family was torn apart. She didn't travel to Little Rock to find her children when she was released. She continued her lifestyle of drugs and homelessness for many more years. She had gone back to prison, last Kyra heard. But keeping tabs on her mother had never been a priority.

Why should she? Deidra was the cause of so much pain in her life, countless hopeless nights. When she was a child, Kyra often wondered why she couldn't have a normal mother, like her friends at school; the kind who packed lunches and made breakfast and dinner and helped them with their homework sometimes.

Instead Kyra had Deidra; the woman who turned their home into a crack house and stalked the streets like a zombie while her children tossed in their beds at night. This was the woman who took her boyfriend's side when Kyra felt she was being sized up for a sexual assault. Donovan was there for her through all of it, and he was still with her now. He was more of a constant in Kyra's life than her mother ever was.

"Mama?"

Duke took a step forward. He didn't run to her with outstretched arms, but he did take a step in her direction, which was more than Kyra was able to do.

Deidra looked embarrassed by all of the attention. She knew she was the black sheep of the family. Almost everyone in the waiting room had cursed her for being a crackhead at some point in time. Only the younger generation, the nieces and nephews, had an empty slate that hadn't been filled with sad stories about Aunt Dee.

"Why y'all looking at me like that?" Deidra must've known that was a ridiculous question. They had every right to regard her like an apparition. She scanned the crowd without making eye contact with most of them, but she did lock eyes with her son and daughter. "What's wrong, Kyra?" She offered a contrite smile.

Donovan took his wife's hand. She grasped and squeezed his tightly.

"I, I didn't expect to see you here," she managed. Her face was void of color. Her mother had become a folktale in her life; a foggy, depressing story that sounded too horrible to be real.

"Why you think I wouldn't come?" Deidra replied. "My baby on her deathbed. Of course I'd come."

"Jessica's gonna be alright," Aunt Joyce said.

She looked her sister up and down and somehow managed to keep a straight face. Deidra was more than a little rough around the edges. She had the nerve to top her tragic ensemble with a jet black wig. Joyce worried for years that she would never see her sister again – except at her inevitable funeral. Deidra was living life so fast, everyone knew it was only a matter of time.

But she wasn't dead. And apparently she still cared about something. The wall of ice that had been erected between the two sisters quickly melted.

"Damn, it's good to see you," Joyce said. She was the first to throw her arms around Deidra and welcome her back into the fold.

Other members of the family followed suit. They greeted Aunt Ruth with the same enthusiasm. She rarely made the trip to Arkansas, so their visit was doubly sweet.

But Kyra hung back, as did her big brother. On the outskirts of the crowd, they eyed each other warily. Both of their spouses stood by them. Donovan had seen Deidra bugged-out, high on cocaine, and Sheryl had heard many repulsive stories from Duke.

Kyra knew she had to talk to her mother. But she didn't know what would happen when she finally had a chance to vocalize all of the pain and heartache this woman had caused her. Their family drama was the stuff of daytime television, but there would be no audience when she and Deidra finally spoke their peace.

● ● ● ● ● ●

Deidra was given priority over the other visitors and was ushered to Jessica's bedside immediately. Kyra remained uncomfortable with Aunt Ruth in the waiting room, but she was cordial enough to tell her, "Hey, Auntie. I'm glad you could make it."

She sat with Donovan and watched as Ruth interacted with the others. She remained the center of attention in Deidra's absence. For Kyra, it was unnerving to see how much everyone loved and missed Ruth. She knew that was because none of them had ever lived with the foul woman. Kyra never told them about the things Ruth did to her when she, Katavia and Quinell sought shelter under her roof.

After a few minutes, she began to feel sick to her stomach. She told Donovan, "Can we leave for a while?"

"Yeah." He stood without question and helped her to her feet.

Before they made it to the elevators, Kyra heard her aunt mention them.

"It's a damn shame we live in the same city, but she couldn't pick up the phone to ask about traveling together..."

Kyra's face burned. She found that comment preposterous. After everything Ruth put her through, she would be the last person Kyra called for *anything* – especially a carpool buddy.

"When'd y'all get in?" Ruth asked them directly.

Kyra didn't turn to face her. Her teeth were clenched, her nostrils flared.

Donovan interceded. "Yesterday, around seven."

"Y'all drove?"

Donovan couldn't believe she was speaking to him casually, as if there was no bad blood between them. The last time he talked to Ruth, she'd lied about Kyra being with another man. She thought she could run Donovan off, but the attempt had the opposite effect.

"No, we flew," he told her.

Ruth's eyes lit up behind her thick-lens glasses. "Hmph. Well, everybody ain't got it like that. Kyra, why you didn't call, to see if we wanted to come with y'all? I know you still got my number."

Kyra squeezed her husband's hand even tighter. Donovan absorbed her frustration.

"I'm sorry Auntie," she said, barely looking back. "I was so scared for Jessica, I didn't think about it."

She continued to walk towards the elevators. Donovan had to follow suit, or she would've dragged him. When they got there, he stared into his wife's eyes as they waited for the lift to arrive. Kyra's cheeks were red. She was fuming.

The moment they stepped onto the elevator, she released his hand and balled hers into fists. She half-growled, half-screamed as they descended to the ground floor.

"I hate her! I can't stand her!" Tears of frustration stung her eyes.

Donovan didn't try to dissuade her from feeling that way. He knew how badly Ruth had treated her. Kat and Q were innocent victims as well. They would probably cry if they ever ran into Ruth again.

Donovan leaned against the wall of the elevator and told Kyra, "You know, you look real sexy when you're mad."

She was so angry, it took a moment to register what he said. Her eyes flashed irritation when they locked on his. "What?"

"I said you look awfully sexy when you're mad," he commented. He folded his arms and bent one leg, propping his foot on the wall behind him.

His demeanor threw her rage off track. She shook her head and frowned. "What does that mean?"

He shrugged. "I don't know. Just saying."

Her eyebrows remained bunched together, but a smile parted her strawberry-colored lips. "What does that have to do with anything?"

"I was wondering what you would do, if I decided to take you, right here on this elevator," he said.

Kyra's frown softened as she contemplated this new quandary. *Take me? On the elevator?*

He pushed off the wall and took a step towards her, giving her even less time to figure things out. But a bell dinged softly as the elevator came to a stop and the doors opened. Donovan grinned as he led her into the lobby.

"What happened to our hotel room?" Kyra asked as they walked down a brightly lit hall that was decorated with bells, ribbons and twinkling lights.

"I told them we wouldn't make it until tonight," Donovan replied.

"When'd you call?"

"Yesterday."

"I didn't notice," she said. But then again, she wasn't aware of many of his plans for this trip.

"Why are you asking about our hotel room?" he wondered.

She grinned. "Why did you say you would take me, right there on the elevator?"

"Because I wanted to take you, on the elevator."

She chuckled. "As much as I love your sense of adventure, I think the hotel would be better."

"I think you're right," he said and pulled his cellphone from his pocket.

"Who you calling?"

"Quinell."

She smiled and nearly melted into a pool of adoration for her husband.

• • • • • •

When they returned to the waiting room, Kyra saw that her mother was now the center of attention, rather than Aunt Ruth. She assumed her aunt was visiting with Jessica. She was surprised to see Duke engaging their mother in conversation. He wasn't smiling though, which could've meant he hadn't decided whether he would forgive her for choosing drugs over her children.

Kyra wished she could speak to her brother, just the two of them, before she had to face their mother alone. But it wasn't meant to be. The moment Deidra saw that she and Donovan were back, she turned in her seat and watched them as they drew nearer. She looked Donovan up and down and smiled. She didn't have the best grin in the world, but only one of her front teeth was fully missing, which was better than Kyra expected.

"You that boy who used to come over all the time, when y'all was kids," she said to Kyra's husband. "Your name's *Donovan*."

He nodded. He returned her smile half-heartedly.

"Y'all done grew up and got married," Deidra said, her smile brightening.

Donovan couldn't help but express delight at that.

"I knew y'all was gon' get married one day," Deidra continued. "Y'all always said you were *just friends*, but I knew better."

Unlike her husband, Kyra didn't like to see Deidra smile and dote on them, like she'd been a loving mother all these years. There were things that needed to be said. She wasn't willing to play get-along-gang until her dear, old ma answered a few poignant questions.

"Can I talk to you?"

The warm, fuzzy mood vanished when everyone saw Kyra's expression. She was a beautiful woman, with innocent features. The anguish behind her big, brown eyes broke her relatives' hearts.

"Yes, we can talk," Deidra said, pushing herself up from her seat. She looked around the waiting room, which was large, but too small for the talk they needed to have. "You wanna go over..."

"Yeah," Kyra said. She turned and headed for the elevators. "We should go..."

• • • • • •

The ride downstairs was tense. Kyra didn't want to start a conversation that might be interrupted if someone joined them on the next floor, so she didn't speak at all. She didn't want to stare at the woman who gave birth to her, so she didn't look at her, either.

When the elevator doors opened on the bottom floor, she stepped off without a word. Deidra followed her. Kyra continued past the spectacularly decorated Christmas tree near the main entrance. She exited the hospital and was greeted by a soft winter breeze. It wasn't noon yet, but the sun was bright in the eastern sky as it rose above the hospital complexes.

Kyra took the steps down to the sidewalk and followed the path as it curved around the building. She didn't realize how quickly she was walking until she noticed her mother struggling to keep up.

"Damn, girl. You said you wanted to talk."

Kyra slowed and allowed Deidra to sidle up to her.

She said, "Sorry," but shot her a look of irritation.

After they had walked a reasonable distance from the main entrance, Deidra sighed and tried to get things moving along.

"What do you want to ask me, Kyra? Why I did drugs? Where I been all these years? Why I didn't try to find y'all? What do you wanna know?"

Kyra frowned. Initially she wasn't sure why that comment upset her. But then she knew.

"Is that how easy it is?" she quipped. "I haven't seen you since I was sixteen, and you wanna run up in here with a bunch of quick answers?"

Deidra shook her head. "Naw, baby. That's not what I meant. I don't have no quick answers."

Kyra also took offense to this woman – this *imposter* – calling her *baby*. Deidra didn't deserve to use that term of endearment. She didn't earn it.

"I said that because that's what's been eating me up over the years," Deidra explained. "I been to counseling. I been to rehab – *a bunch of times*. That's what they said I'd have to answer whenever I got to see my children again. Y'all would wanna know where I been, and why I did it."

Kyra still didn't like the ease into which they'd broached these questions. She always hoped this conversation would be like pulling teeth. She wanted her mother to break down and cry and beg for forgiveness. But the counselors were right. Those were the questions that tormented her the most.

"So, where have you been?" she asked.

"On the streets," Deidra said matter-of-factly. "You know that."

Kyra did. "You still smoke crack?"

Deidra nodded.

Kyra was disappointed that a woman in her late fifties would admit to such a thing, but she appreciated the honesty.

"Why can't you stop?"

Her mother shrugged. She had an exhausted, defeated look in her eyes. "I tried a bunch of times, Kyra. You know that. I tried when y'all was little. I tried when I went to prison. I just did another six months in rehab last year. I been trying my whole life. I'll try again tomorrow, if you want me to."

Kyra balked at that. "If *I* want you to?"

"That's another problem I got," Deidra informed her. "It's a whole lot easier *not* to try, when don't nobody care if you try or not."

Her daughter gave her an incredulous look. "So you're blaming me for your problems?"

"Naw." Deidra frowned and waved that off. "I'm just telling you how it is. I done burned so many bridges in my lifetime, I don't expect nobody to help me. Once you get to my age and have been to jail as many times as me, people expect you to keep on a certain route. That's my life. It don't mean I don't love you – all of you. But I don't expect for y'all to love me back. It's better if I just stay outta the way. Y'all did better without me around."

"No," Kyra shook her head. Tears filled her eyes as she considered all of the terrible turns her life took when her mom went to prison. "We needed you. We had to move to Arkansas. I barely finished school. I watched people get killed. Q's dad…"

The tears rolled down her cheeks. She remembered holding Quinell's father in her arms as he bled out on her grandmother's couch.

"I know about that, and I'm sorry," Deidra said. To her credit, she looked genuinely remorseful. "But you were living with a mother who was on drugs. You can't tell me I raised you better than your grandmama did. I should've been there for y'all. I should've got clean. I know it. But your life turned out better without me in it. Despite everything you went through, look at you now. Look at Duke, and Jessica. All y'all have *good* lives. You made me proud."

Kyra hated that Deidra could be so wrong about everything, yet somehow right at the same time. In a perfect world, her mother would've gotten clean and raised her family right. Failing that, removing her crack addiction from her children's lives probably was the best thing Deidra could do for them.

"Why didn't you come see us when you got out of jail?" she asked as she wiped the tears from her face.

"Girl, do you know how hard it is for a crackhead to book a trip to Little Rock?" Deidra ventured. "I can't tell you how many times I had the money in hand, with full intentions of buying me a bus ticket. But before I made it downtown, I'd run into one of my friends, and we'd get to talking, and the next thing I know I spent my bus money on dope. I can't tell you how many times that happened." She chuckled.

Kyra shook her head.

"Why you ain't never try to find me?" Deidra wondered. "You came back to Overbrook Meadows three years ago."

"I did find you," her daughter stated. "Me and Donovan tracked you down to the Union Gospel Mission."

Deidra was surprised to hear that.

"We got there in the morning one day," Kyra continued. "We saw you with some tall, bald-headed man. You had two sack lunches, and y'all looked happy. Seemed like your life was going just fine. I didn't want to bother you."

Deidra smiled. "That must'a been *Fred*. That man was so tall, he could jump a fence without jumping. One of the biggest con artists I know," she mused. "He talked me out of making that trip to Little Rock plenty of times. Took me straight to the dope man!" She laughed.

Despite it all, Kyra found herself amused. She wondered if this was the type of relationship she could expect, if she allowed her mother to become a part of her life. Deidra would regale them with strange stories from the hood, and she'd come up missing sometimes until she inevitably came up missing for the *final time*, and they got a call from the police.

Or maybe it didn't have to end like that. Deidra was pushing sixty. Maybe she'd be willing to give up drugs for good someday soon. At this point, Kyra refused to get her hopes up. But it wasn't completely farfetched.

"So what happens now?" Deidra asked. Apparently she'd been thinking along the same lines. "Are you gonna let me see my grandbabies sometime, or do you want me to crawl back under my rock, over by the shelter?"

"I don't want you to crawl back under a rock," Kyra told her. "I'll give you my number. If you're ever feeling *exceptionally sober* one day, I'll come get you and bring you to the house."

"*Exceptionally sober*? What that mean?"

"Like you haven't been high at all that day."

"Oh, well, you have to catch me in the morning then," Deidra said with another one of her cackling laughs.

Kyra shook her head, but she couldn't help but smile. "No, I'm not gonna try to track you down, Mama. You call me if you want to come by. If not, I'll understand."

Deidra became quiet for a moment. That was the first time Kyra had called her *Mama* in a very long time.

"Okay, baby. I understand what you're saying."

"But don't ever call me for money," Kyra added.

"I wouldn't do that," Deidra said. She sounded slightly offended.

"I hope not, but I do need to make that clear," Kyra said.

"That's fine," Deidra said. "I haven't asked you for money in seventeen years. What makes you think I'ma start now?"

"You haven't had my number in seventeen years," Kyra pointed out. "Or I'm sure you would've!"

They both laughed at that.

"How does it feel to come home after all that time and find Donovan waiting for you?" Deidra asked when they quieted down.

Kyra knew that Donovan wasn't exactly waiting for her when she returned to Overbrook Meadows. He was actually involved with a beautiful woman named Brianna at the time.

But she smiled and told her mother, "It was wonderful. It was the best thing ever."

● ● ● ● ● ●

Kyra and Donovan stayed at the hospital for the rest of the day, until the sun began to dip behind the hulking hospital towers. Before they left, they visited with Jessica again and were happy to see her holding her baby. Her cheeks and lips had more color, and her mind was free of sedatives. There was laughter and happy hearts in her room.

Jessica waved her little sister over while Uncle Harold discussed plans the family was making for Christmas.

Kyra approached her bedside with a smile. Jessica gestured for her to lean closer.

She did, and her sister told her, "Did you know I died while I was having this baby?"

Kyra frowned, and her smile faltered a bit. "Yeah, I knew that," she said softly.

"That's why you came; y'all thought I was gonna die. Everybody did."

Kyra shook her head. "Nah," she said with a grin. "We knew you were gonna be alright. We prayed for you."

Jessica bit her bottom lip. Kyra didn't know if she had just learned what happened or if she was finally reacting to it. Hearing that your heart wasn't beating for almost a whole television commercial can be a sobering experience.

"This little joker tried to take me out," she said.

The troublemaker in question was asleep in her arms. Even in slumber, it was clear Gary Jr. loved the sound of his mother's voice. The child was fully at peace.

Kyra smiled. "But you gotta forgive him, though. Him so *cute*."

"Yeah," Jessica agreed. "I don't think I would be able to take that from an ugly baby."

"Girl, you know you wrong for that!"

"I love you," Jessica said with a sigh. "Thanks for coming."

"You know I love you, too," Kyra told her.

"What'd you think of Mama showing up?" Jessica asked her. "When I saw her, I thought I was looking at a ghost."

Kyra nodded. "Me too. I don't know what to think about her. I guess I'm glad to see her. At least we know she's still alive."

"Yeah," Jessica agreed. "I doubt if she'll ever come back to Little Rock, but you got a better chance of running into her in Overbrook Meadows. Did she tell you where she lives?"

"I already know she lives at the homeless shelter."

"Are you gonna start, you know, trying to be around her and stuff?" Jessica wondered.

"She said she's gonna make an effort to be in our lives," Kyra reported. "I gave her my number. But I'm not gonna go looking for her if she doesn't call."

"Did you tell her how ridiculous that wig looked?" Jessica inquired.

Kyra laughed at that. "No. I couldn't tell her that."

"Shit, I did," Jessica told her. "It's bad enough she a crackhead. She don't have to walk around looking like one!"

CHAPTER SEVEN
BEST WIFE EVER

The faint smell of your perfume
Your body pressed so close to mine
I hold you as our kiss resumes
Our bodies soon are intertwined
A kiss
One kiss
Your lips
Those hips
So full
So soft
So sweet
So deep

On the way to their hotel room, Kyra called Ms. Beverly while Donovan drove.

"Hey, Kyra! I hear your sister's doing better!"

"She is," Kyra beamed. "She's back to her old self. She's been holding the baby and everything."

"She's holding the baby?"

"Yeah. She got her strength back. That is one cute baby! Did Donovan send you a picture?"

"No. Do you mind sending one?"

"No. I don't mind."

"When are y'all coming back?"

"Maybe tomorrow. But I want to see a few more people here before we go. And I want to make sure my sister is okay."

"No rush," Beverly said. "But you know the kids have been worried about y'all missing Christmas."

"We won't. We'll make sure to be back in time."

"Quinell's reaching for the phone," Beverly told her. "You wanna talk to him?"

"Sure."

A moment later the boy came to the line.

"Mama?"

Hearing her son's voice made Kyra's heart swell with affection. "Hey, Q!"

"Mama, when are y'all coming home? Are you gonna be here for Christmas?"

Kyra found his persistence humorous. This reminded her of the time Donovan promised to take them to Six Flags. Q questioned whether the plans were still valid every day for a week leading up to Saturday.

"Yes, we'll be home for Christmas," she promised him.

"Tomorrow's Christmas *Eve*," Q pointed out. "You have to leave by tomorrow to get back in time."

"No, we're flying back," she told him. "We can leave Christmas morning and be home in a couple of hours."

"But you'll get stuck at the airport," the boy worried. "A lot of people are stuck at the airport. It was on the news."

"Our flight will be fine. There's no snow here, so there's no ice at the airport. Aren't you having a good time with your grandmother?"

"Yeah, but we won't be able to get our presents, if y'all don't come back in time."

Kyra rolled her eyes, still smiling. The boy may have missed her and Donovan, but Christmas presents were his top priority.

"I already told you Santa can find you wherever you are."

"Come on, Mama."

"How's Doc and Wyatt?" Donovan asked.

"Donovan wants to know how the dogs are," Kyra reported.

"They're fine. You can tell they miss us, though. They get real excited when I go back there to feed them."

"They're fine," Kyra told her husband.

"Does he spend a little time with them when he feeds them?" Donovan asked.

"Here," Kyra said, passing him the phone.

Donovan took it and said, "Hey, Q? Do you spend time with the dogs, when you go by to feed them? They need food, but they need play time, too."

Kyra leaned back in her seat and enjoyed the ride as he continued the conversation.

● ● ● ● ● ●

When they got to their hotel room, Kyra called first dibs on the shower. Donovan didn't complain, though he was just as eager to feel the spray of warm water.

Kyra didn't mean to take long, but the shower felt so good she could've fallen asleep standing up. She felt soothed and refreshed when she got out, as if all of her stress from the past 24 hours had swirled down the drain with the soapy water.

She didn't bring a robe, so she stepped out of the bathroom with a towel wrapped around her body.

"It's all yours."

Those words were like music to Donovan's ears, but he couldn't step by his wife without admiring her glow and imagining the wonders that were hidden beneath her towel.

Kyra had her hair pulled up and tied loosely, leaving a couple of tresses dangling over her face. Her lips were full and pink, her face free of make-up. She had her towel pulled over her breasts, but that left the bottom portion precariously short. Less than two inches of fabric hung past the intersection between her thighs.

Donovan went to her and kissed her softly. Kyra smiled as she returned the love. He pressed forward until her backside encountered the bathroom sink. He deepened the kiss, reaching for the spot where the towel was tucked in. When he found it, he pulled the fabric, and it fell away loosely.

Kyra stood totally nude. The look in her husband's eyes and the feel of his hands on her sides heated her more than the shower had.

He backed away and grinned appreciatively as he looked her up and down. Kyra was sinfully voluptuous. Donovan felt blood rushing to his manhood as his eyes devoured her full breasts and dark nipples. The sight of her pubic hair made his nostrils flare slightly. When his gaze returned to her eyes, he saw how exhausted she was. They were only able to snag a few hours of good sleep the night before, when they dozed on the couch in the waiting room.

"You're tired," he said. "Are you going to bed?"

Sleep was one of her body's most pressing needs, but she looked down and saw the bulge in his boxers. She smirked. "No. I'll wait for you."

"Alright," he said and began to disrobe before he stepped into the shower.

Kyra watched him for a moment, long enough to get a pleasing look at his bare ass, before she left the bathroom. She found panties and a bra in her suitcase but didn't think she'd need them tonight. She opted for only a nightgown.

Donovan meant to hurry in the shower – he thought he had – but when he emerged from the steamy bathroom, he realized he'd been in there for more than ten minutes. The bath was as dreamy as Kyra made it seem. His body felt loose and drained.

When he spotted his wife on the bed, he smiled as he bent to pull the covers over her. Kyra said she'd wait for him, but her fatigued brain said otherwise. She looked to be already in the deep, dream stage of sleep.

There were still suitcases on the bed. Donovan set them aside and turned off the lights. He crawled under the sheets and was greeted by his wife's lovely warmth. He scooted forward until his chest pressed against her back. She backed into him impulsively. Their bodies fit together like a puzzle. With her wonderful ass in his lap, Donovan's manhood began to respond again. But his brain shut everything down before he reached a full erection.

● ● ● ● ● ●

The sleep was better than the shower.
The wakening was better than both.

"Roll over," Kyra said, helping to position him on his back.

Donovan opened his eyes, a little, enough to see there was sunlight and Kyra, hovering over him.

"Why didn't you wake me up?" she asked as she pulled his boxers down.

Donovan didn't know what was going on, but even his subconscious knew there was never anything wrong with his wife taking his boxers off. He reached and helped her with them.

"When?" he muttered.

"Last night, when you got out the shower."

"You were sleep," he breathed, his eyes squeezed closed against the sunlight.

"You should've woke me up," she said as she took hold of his manhood. "You make me feel like a bad wife." She squeezed and stroked him, bringing him to half-mast within seconds.

Donovan opened his eyes and looked down in time to see his dick disappear inside her mouth. His eyes grew large, and his toes curled. His erection reached its full potential after only a few bobs of her head. Kyra's mouth was a warm, wet paradise. Her lips were sensual. Her tongue was magical. He saw that she was completely nude, as was he.

She looked up at him, which sometimes made him feel self-conscious, but Donovan was learning to relax and enjoy everything about the experience.

Her mouth moved up and off his pole, and she asked, "I'm not a bad wife, am I?"

Donovan found the question outrageous, especially now, as she spoke against his dick like a microphone. Her breaths on his sensitive skin made him jump in her fist.

"No," he managed. "You're a great wife. The best ever."

Kyra's eyes slipped closed and she smiled, as if his reply truly meant the world to her. Donovan's heart thundered. She devoured him again. His toes curled again, and he wondered what he'd done to deserve such a wonderful wake-up call. The sound of her sucking made his stomach tighten. The light to medium pressure of her jaws was mind-numbing.

He felt like a king as he watched her. This was paradise. But he wasn't upset when his queen came up for air. She crawled over him until her bare chest was level with his. He felt the heat of her opening radiating over his hardness, and then she lowered herself, inviting him to invade her slick walls.

"*Uhhh-hmmm.*" She hummed as he spread her and made himself at home.

For her, this position could be used for dominance. But at this moment, her only goal was to pleasure him. Every rock of her hips and squeeze of her thighs was designed to bring him to a state of marital bliss and sexual fulfillment. Her breasts pressed against him as she slowly grinded her hips.

He reached and caressed her thighs. He squeezed her ass, pushing his hips off the bed until he had all of her. When he came down, their thighs clapped, and she began to grind harder, ensuring he hit the deepest spot – the sweetest spot – every time.

She pushed up and placed both hands on his chest. Her hips moved faster now, back and forth. Her breasts bounced in his face. The look on her face was ecstasy personified. Donovan wished he could touch and kiss everything; all at the same time. He wished he could enjoy her longer, but he was near surrender. And she knew it.

"Tell me I'm a good wife," she breathed.

"You're a good wife," he said, obediently, without hesitation. "You're the best wife ever."

She smiled that sublime smile again; the one that made him believe his validation meant the world to her. She began to rock her hips with a seductive rhythm that made her ass jiggle. Donovan closed his eyes and grunted as her efforts to please him were rewarded. She felt him jumping inside her, and she welcomed his seed. Her heart skipped a beat as her walls contracted, and her clitoris bestowed its offering.

She collapsed on top of him. Their love mingled. Donovan had lost much of his strength, but he refused to let go of her ass as her hips continued to rock back and forth for another blessed minute.

• • • • • •

That day Kyra wanted to spend more time with her relatives before she and Donovan headed home on Christmas morning. He wasn't opposed to that, especially after the wonders of their lovemaking that morning.

They went to the hospital and were thrilled to see Jessica on her feet, walking around her unit.

"I gotta get out of here," she said.

"How come?" Kyra asked.

"I hate hospitals," Jessica stated. "I'm sick of nurses and techs coming in my room all times of the day; taking my temperature and stuff. And don't get me wrong, I love my family, but I'm sick of seeing some of them too. They just walk in my room whenever they feel like it. If I was at home, I could turn off the lights and play sleep, but that doesn't work up in here. Even when I do play sleep, they just sit there and stare at me."

Kyra found that hilarious. "I can't believe you're mad because people love and care about you."

"It's mostly the hospital," Jessica told her. "This place is for sick people. I'm not sick."

Kyra saw that her health had significantly improved over the last couple of days.

"Where's Gary?" she asked.

"Home with the baby."

"They let the baby go?"

"Yeah. He got discharged yesterday."

"Really? I saw Gary here with him last night."

"He was just visiting," Jessica told her. "They spent the night, but I don't want my baby up here with all these sick people. I think Gary's taking him to visit his side of the family today. They'll be back later on."

"Has the doctor said when you can go home?" Kyra asked her.

"Either tonight or tomorrow morning."

"So you'll be home for Christmas. That's good."

"Oh, I'll definitely be home for Christmas," Jessica said as her walk ended back where it began; in her hospital room. "Even if I have to leave AMA, I'll be home for Christmas."

"What's AMA?"

"*Against medical advice*," Jessica explained. "That's what these nurses keep telling me when I say I'm about to go: '*You can't leave AMA, or your insurance won't cover it!*'"

Kyra laughed at the way her sister mimicked her caregivers.

"What's up with y'all?" Jessica asked. "Why you look so happy today?"

Donovan raised an eyebrow. He felt as if she knew about the marital activities they were engaged in that morning.

Kyra said, "We didn't have to spend the night here yesterday. That's enough to make anybody happy."

"Are y'all going home today?"

"No. Our flight's tomorrow morning. We're gonna visit some folks before we hit the road."

"Can you bring me some chicken for dinner?" Jessica asked.

"Sure," Kyra said. "Is it okay for you to eat it here?"

"Yeah, I don't have any food restrictions. You can ask my nurse."

"Okay. Do you know where Mama and Aunt Ruth are?"

"I think they were supposed to spend the night at Grandmama's house."

Kyra's grandmother passed away fifteen years ago and left the house to Uncle Harold. But as far as the family was concerned, it would always be *Grandmama's house.*

"Okay, we'll be back by dinnertime," Kyra promised her. "Is Gary bringing the baby back? I can't leave without seeing my nephew again."

"He'll be here," Jessica told her. Before her visitors took off, she said, "Hey, Donovan."

They both turned back to her.

"I said *Donovan*," Jessica stated, and then she spoke to him directly. "Thank you for always being there for my sister, ever since y'all were kids."

This was the second time she told him that. The first time was when she came to Overbrook Meadows for their wedding.

Donovan said, "You don't have to thank me for that. I love Kyra. She's a wonderful wife."

Kyra beamed while he sister said, "Yeah, yeah. You think the sun revolves around her. But I know it wasn't easy to come to Arkansas and get all this history thrown at you – especially when our mama showed up. Some people might think my sister has a lot of baggage. But you never did. You changed her life."

Donovan never expected any accolades for helping Kyra reach her potential. Even when they were children, he didn't like to get a pat on the back for doing the right thing.

"She changed my life as much as I've changed hers," he replied. "I'm loving every minute of it."

"*Ugh!*" Jessica fake-gagged. "I see y'all still living a fairy tale. Didn't the honeymoon phase wear off by now?"

Kyra found that comical. Jessica had no idea what it took for her and Donovan to reach this level of contentment in their marriage.

"It does feel like a fairy tale," she said and took her husband's hand.

"...With a happily ever after," Donovan agreed.

The happy couple kissed and left the room, before Jessica found something to throw at them.

● ● ● ● ● ●

The not-so-newlyweds spent the rest of the day exploring Kyra's old stomping grounds. Donovan knew that she'd left a bad neighborhood in Overbrook Meadows only to move to an even worse ghetto in Little Rock. But it wasn't as bad as he'd imagined. He might have had a different opinion at nighttime, but during the day he only saw regular poor people who were trying to enjoy life while living with less.

They visited Aunt Joyce, who was off work for the holidays. Kyra got a chance to get to know her boyfriend William. He was a seasoned plumber who was looking to start his own company. Joyce made taco salad for lunch. Kyra enjoyed visiting with her cousins Tevin and Kevin, who had just graduated from high school. Back when she lived with her aunt, the boys were in diapers. It was great to see that they had grown into strong, educated black men.

Kyra and Donovan stopped by her brother's house next. Duke's wife forced them to eat even more food; this time it was a sweet potato pie she needed someone to taste-test before she made several more for Christmas. All of Duke's children were there. Kyra caught up with her nieces while Donovan joined Melvin and Duke in the garage. They'd been tinkering with an old Mustang for nearly a year. Duke promised to hand the muscle car down to his son when they got it up and running.

When they left her brother's house, Kyra directed Donovan to her grandmother's, where she had also lived for a little while. The home became a sad, lonely place after her Granny died, but it was now bustling with life and love. Uncle Harold had a huge family. And Kyra's mom and aunt were there. She avoided Ruth for the next two hours and had a great time with everyone else.

At six o'clock she told Donovan, "Don't forget, we have to get Jessica some chicken."

"I haven't forgotten."

"How you holding up?" she asked him. "Are you bored."

"No, not at all. But I can't keep eating like this!"

It took a few minutes to leave the house, because everyone wanted to hug them goodbye.

Deidra told her, "Don't forget, I'm gonna call you when I get back, so I can see my grandbabies!"

"Okay, Mama." Kyra gave her a big hug and a kiss on the cheek. She hoped Deidra would call, but she didn't put too much faith in it.

As they backed out of Uncle Harold's driveway, Donovan said, "Your old neighborhood doesn't seem so bad."

Kyra continued to smile radiantly. She'd been in good spirits since she made love to him that morning. "I never said it was *all* bad. But it was bad, a lot of the time."

Donovan knew that Quinell's father had been stabbed to death in the living room they just vacated, but he didn't want his wife to dwell on those memories.

"Everybody misses you a lot. We should visit more often."

"Really?" Her eyes brightened. "That would be awesome! They all want to see Q and Kat."

"We can come in the summer," Donovan offered, "when we get our time off from school."

Kyra reached to hold his free hand while he drove. She leaned over and kissed him on the cheek.

"Thank you, baby. I love you."

Not for the first time, Donovan was taken aback by how easy it was to please her. Some guys had to buy expensive jewelry to get a similar reaction. He didn't think married life could be this simple. But after two and a half years, Kyra had remained the same sweet woman he wed.

They took a ten piece chicken dinner to the hospital. Unfortunately it wasn't enough for everyone. Gary and the baby were back along with Jessica's other two children and a host of relatives from both sides of the family. Donovan gave the food to the patient and let her decide who she wanted to share with. Initially, Jessica didn't want to share with *anyone*.

By the time they left the hospital, Kyra's heart was full with familial love. A part of her had dreaded returning to Little Rock, even for something as dire as her sister's brush with death. But after facing the ghosts from her past, she felt stronger for the experience.

Next to her sister getting better, Kyra's favorite part about the trip was showing off her wonderful husband. From the moment she said "I do," she knew she had found the best lover, provider, protector and friend in the world. It was gratifying to know that everyone in her family agreed with her.

CHAPTER EIGHT
THE FINAL CHAPTER
'TIS CHRISTMAS DAY!

I feel your heart as we lay close
An erotic river begins to flow
I gently caress your hips and thighs
Then spread your lips and slide inside
You cry out as I raise your knees
I shudder from the ecstasy

The next morning Donovan awakened to an empty bed. His wife was on the phone in the living area adjacent to the bedroom. He rose quickly and checked to make sure she was seated in the front room before he rummaged through his luggage for a surprise.

By the time Kyra got off the phone, he had brushed his teeth and was packing up the clothes and toiletries they brought on the trip. Kyra found him wearing only boxers when she returned to the bedroom.

"Good morning!" she sang.

She hadn't changed out of her nightgown, but she was fully awake and obviously excited.

"Good morning," Donovan replied. "Merry Christmas!"

"Merry Christmas, baby!"

She stepped to him and threw her arms around his neck. They pretended there was a sprig of mistletoe overhead. Donovan's hands traveled down her sides and found a home on her plump derriere. He squeezed and pulled her hips closer, causing a mellow heat to flow down Kyra's body. She closed her eyes and hugged him tightly.

"I can't wait to get home," she murmured.

"Me, too. Did you talk to your sister?"

"Yeah," she said as they separated. "That was her."

"Did she get discharged yet?"

Kyra nodded. "Yep. They let her go about an hour ago. She's already home; spending Christmas with her family."

"Do you want to stop by there before we head to the airport?"

"No. We don't have to. What times' our flight?"

"Ten-thirty."

"Good," she said. "We might make it home before the kids wake up."

"Yeah, right." Donovan shook his head. "Judging by how excited they are, I'm surprised they're not calling already."

"Why do you think Q's so excited this year?" Kyra wondered.

"I don't know. It might be because he doesn't believe in Santa anymore," Donovan guessed as he continued packing.

"Why would that make him more excited?"

"Because his wish list isn't going to some stranger who may or may not get him what he wants. He knows we're doing the shopping, and we love him, so his chances are a lot better." He chuckled.

Kyra loved to hear Donovan speak of the kids as if he was their biological father. Not all step-fathers could do that. It was a little thing for some women, but for her it was huge.

"I don't like that he doesn't believe anymore," she said, taking a seat on the bed.

"He's almost eleven. How long did you think he'd believe in Santa?"

"At least until he's a teenager."

Donovan grinned. "You want him to believe some kook from the North Pole is flying around giving away free gifts?"

"Santa's not a kook," she said, slapping his arm playfully. "There's nothing wrong with a child believing in Christmas magic. It's fun."

Donovan agreed that it was. Some of his fondest holiday memories were from the days he believed the gifts under the Christmas tree showed up miraculously while he slept. It was a bit of a letdown to know that it was actually his parents – but that never took away from his enjoyment of the presents.

"Speaking of Santa, I got you something," he said and reached under his pillow.

"Oh no!" Kyra's hands flew to her face. "I didn't get you anything!"

"Really? You suck," Donovan said, and didn't retrieve her gift.

"I know! I'm sorry." Her frown was more cute than serious. "I have something for you at home, but I didn't want to pack it. I didn't want to add more weight to my bag."

"For real? How big is it?" he wondered. "Did you get those fishing poles I've been hinting at?"

"You were hinting at fishing poles?"

"Yeah. I said I'd like to take Q out to the lake one morning."

"You said that *one time*!"

"So I'm guessing you didn't get me fishing poles..."

"Baby, you're making me feel worse," she pouted. "Come here."

She pulled him closer by tugging the front of his boxers.

"You can't solve all of our problems like that," he joked.

"Yes I can. You said I sucked. Let's see."

She grabbed hold of his meat through his undies, and Donovan had a quick change of heart. This was an excellent way to settle this!

"Wait, let me show you what I got you first." He stepped away and reached under his pillow again. He returned with a small gift bag from one of her favorite jewelers.

"Oh my God!" she exclaimed. "You went to Jared!"

Donovan laughed. She sounded like their advertisement. "Sorry, I didn't have time to wrap them individually."

"*Them*?" She dug into the bag and produced two jewelry boxes; one large and one small. She popped the rectangular box open first. Inside was a gorgeous diamond solitaire sitting on a bed of black felt. Kyra brought a hand to her mouth and stared at the necklace with wide, unblinking eyes.

"Oh my – wow – *Donovan*. This is beautiful!"

"Open the other one," he said, standing proudly in his boxers.

Kyra's hands were trembling. She placed the necklace on the bed and pried open the smaller box. This one contained a pair of diamond earrings that matched the necklace.

She gasped, her eyes filling with tears.

"You said Mrs. Ruffin looked *elegant* in her jewelry at our Christmas party," Donovan reminded her. "You said you always wanted to wear jewelry like hers, but you never felt like a diamonds kind of girl."

Mrs. Ruffin was the principal at J. T. Elder, where Kyra worked as an office clerk. She did remember saying that, but, "We missed the Christmas party this year. It was two days ago."

"That's right," Donovan agreed. "You told me that *last* year. Sorry, it took me a while to save up."

Kyra couldn't believe that not only did he pick up on such a vague comment, but he remembered it a whole year later. She felt even worse for not realizing he wanted a set of fishing poles.

"Now, Mrs. Mitchell," he said, "we have an hour before we need to leave for the airport. I would like to see you in your new jewelry – and nothing else." He reached to wipe the tears that were now spilling from her eyes. "Baby, don't cry."

"I – I can't help it," she said. "This is amazing, Donovan. It's crazy."

"Why is it crazy?"

"That you love me so much," she managed. "I don't deserve it. I don't deserve you."

"Don't ever say that. We're meant to be together, Kyra. I'd be nothing without you."

She knew that wasn't the case. But Donovan believed it to be true, which made her heart swell even more.

He bent to kiss her. Her head spun as she got lost in the sensation of his lips and his love and this glorious Christmas morning.

"Wait," she said as he leaned into her, causing her to lie back on the bed.

"Baby, I was just kidding about wearing those," he said. "You're perfect the way you are."

"No, it's not that." She sat up, setting her gifts aside. "I just realized I do have something for you. It's in my bag."

"I don't want some old, wannabe gift," he told her. "I've seen everything in your bag, and I know none of it's for me."

"You didn't see this," she said smiling.

She rolled to her stomach and crawled across the bed. Her bag was on the other side. She felt the mattress sink as Donovan pursued her.

"Where you going?"

He grabbed hold of her legs and pulled her back to him.

"No, seriously," Kyra said laughing. "This isn't really a *Christmas* gift, but I did want to surprise you."

She got moving again. Donovan reached for her hips this time. He stood up on his knees and pulled her into his lap. He pushed her nightie up past the small of her back.

"This is perfect," he said, admiring the view.

"Baby, let me get this."

She dropped to her stomach and began to scramble again. Donovan grabbed hold of her panties and let her go. But she had to leave the underwear behind. She reached over the bed while he stared at her bare ass. It was nice and plump. His dick began to stretch the fabric of his boxers. He removed them and pursued the object of his desire. But Kyra rolled onto her back at that moment, and he saw that she did have something in her hand. Donovan had something in his hand, too.

"What are you doing?" She giggled.

He let go of his dick and reached to spread her caramel thighs. Nothing was better than the gift he found between them – but he was curious about what she was holding. "What's that?"

She offered it to him. All thoughts of sex momentarily left his mind as he stared at it. She had knitted him a sock – except there were a few obvious things wrong with that assertion. First of all, Kyra didn't knit. Secondly, the sock was much too small for him. Maybe it could fit his big toe. The third and most important thing he noticed was it wasn't a sock at all. It was shaped like a little boot. Donovan wasn't an expert on babies, but he was pretty sure it was called a *bootie*.

His heart and mind became jumbled as he tried to respond. He stared and blinked in confusion. Kyra smiled and waited for him to get it out.

"You're pregnant?"

She nodded, her lips pressed closed. She wasn't sure why, but she felt anxious about how he would respond. Kat and Q were already a handful.

Donovan took the bootie from her and continued to inspect it, as if he might find their future son or daughter hidden inside.

He smiled, which caused Kyra to smile as well.

"We're having a baby?"

Her face flushed with heat. Her whole body did. She nodded.

"I'm having a baby?" Donovan's smile grew by degrees. His eyes twinkled like the brightly colored lights on the hospital's Christmas tree.

"Oh baby, this is awesome!" He kissed her excitedly. "This is the best gift ever!"

Kyra was so happy, she felt like she could float right out of the bed. Her thundering heartbeats sounded like applause. Donovan continued to plant soft kisses on her lips as he settled between her legs. Kyra forgot they were naked until he reached down and guided himself into her wet warmth in one smooth motion.

"Oh. *Ooh, baby...*"

She sucked air between her teeth and stared over his massive shoulder. A glorious fire erupted around her clitoris as he pumped his hips slowly, filling her up as only he could. She loved every position, when it came to making love to her husband, but his missionary slow grind was the best. His strokes were short and deep, as if he couldn't bear to slide out more than a couple of inches before each plunge.

He supported himself on his forearms and stared into her eyes as he pushed in deeper and deeper. Kyra felt him in every one of her blood cells. She felt him in her soul.

"I'm about to make a twin up in here," Donovan grunted.

The implausibility of his comment didn't matter at the moment. His loving felt so good, Kyra did not doubt that his seed was magical.

"*Mmmm. Go for it, baby,*" she breathed as her eyes slipped closed. A content smile parted her lips.

Donovan hooked one of her legs in the crook of his arm and began to stroke with more intensity.

"*Damn...*" he muttered. "I think I'm about to make *triplets!*"

EPILOGUE
A CHRISTMAS MIRACLE

The flight home was a lot better than the first one. Kyra was more relaxed because she knew her sister was doing well. And Donovan may have been seven months away from having his first child, but he was already a proud papa. He even told their stewardess, "We're having a baby!" when she commented on his chipper mood.

When the plane touched down in Overbrook Meadows, his phone started ringing the moment he turned it on. Donovan saw his mother's name on the Caller ID, but he knew it wasn't her calling.

"Good morning, Q! Merry Christmas!"

"This not Q. This Kat," the little girl said.

Donovan didn't know the four year old knew how to work a cellphone. "Oh. Well good morning to you, too."

"Mebby Cristhmas! I miss you."

She was so sweet, Donovan could've died from a cuteness overload. He laughed. "Merry Christmas, Katavia! I miss you, too. We'll be there in a little bit."

"Here Q," she said and passed the phone over.

"Donovan?" the boy said.

"Morning, Q. Merry Christmas!"

"Merry Christmas! When are y'all coming home?"

"Our plane just landed," he told him. "We'll be there in an hour and a half."

"Really? Cool. Grandma wanted to know if y'all would make it for dinner."

Donovan knew his mother liked to serve Christmas dinner at one. He checked his watch. "We'll be right on time."

"Okay, cool!" The boy barely took the phone away from his face before yelling, "Grandma, he said they'll be here right on time!"

Donovan heard his mother reply, "Wonderful!"

"I miss y'all," Q told him.

"We miss y'all too," Donovan said. "See you in a little bit."

Leaving the airport on Christmas morning was a little more hectic than they hoped, but nothing could steal their joy, especially after the news of Kyra's pregnancy.

When they made it back to Overbrook Meadows, Donovan told her he wanted to stop by their house before they went to his mother's. She was surprised by that. She was even more confused when they got there, and he told her not to bring in any of their luggage.

"I don't want Q to know we came here first," he explained.

Kyra followed him inside with a puzzled expression, but a minute later everything became clear. She realized, not for the first time, that her husband was a genius. Not only that, but he was an awesome father and provider. There weren't many men who would go through so much just to keep a dream alive.

Fifteen minutes later they arrived at his mother's house in time for her Christmas meal. Most of Donovan's family was from Dallas. He was happy to see that a good number of them had taken Beverly up on her invitation. Ever since his father died, he worried about his mother spending so much time alone, especially during the holidays.

But today she wouldn't have that problem. Aunt Evelyn was there with her whole family, and Uncle Jimmy brought his wife and their six children. Beverly was the perfect hostess. She served all of the traditional favorites.

She noticed Donovan getting anxious towards the end of the meal when someone took the last slice of pecan pie. She told him, "Don't worry, baby. You know I made another one for you to take home. It's in the kitchen."

She winked at him across the table, and he smiled with relief.

After dinner the guests gathered in the living room for music and drinks and an exchange of gifts. Donovan was surprised to see that his mother had something under the tree for everyone. He hadn't seen her so happy in a few years. He didn't feel bad when his group decided to leave at four, because she still had a house full of people.

"I'm so glad everything turned out okay in Little Rock," she told him as he gave her a hug on her doorstep.

In the driveway, Kyra and the kids were piling into his truck.

"Me too," Donovan said. He looked back to make sure Kat and Q weren't listening before he told her, "I got some good news."

"What's that?" Beverly asked.

Her eyes were twinkling. His were, too.

"We didn't want to say anything during dinner, because we haven't told the kids yet," Donovan stated. "But Kyra's finally gonna give you that grandbaby you've been asking for."

The astonished look on his mother's face was priceless. Her smile was as bright as the Christmas lights adorning her home.

"Oh, baby, that's awesome! That's the best Christmas gift ever!"

She hugged him again so tightly Donovan nearly lost his breath – which was quite a feat, considering he was nearly two feet taller and outweighed her by a hundred pounds.

Beverly had tears in her eyes when they separated. She clasped her hands together and giggled with joy.

"Is it a boy or a girl?"

"I don't know, Mama. She's only a couple of months pregnant."

"Ooh, I can't wait!" Beverly said. Her mind began to run wild with grand plans she had for her son's first biological child.

"Okay, Mama, I'll call you later," Donovan said. "Thanks again for keeping the kids for us."

When he joined his family in the truck, Kyra saw that Beverly remained on the porch watching them. Her expression was dreamy. Kyra smiled and waved at her.

"You told her, didn't you?"

"I had to," Donovan said. "I couldn't keep it in."

Kyra wasn't surprised or upset with him. Her husband was a mama's boy through and through. That was one of many things she loved about him.

"Told her what?" Q asked from the backseat.

"Quit being nosey," Kyra joked.

"I wanna know," the boy said.

Donovan told him, "We'll talk about it when we get home."

"We need to talk about what happened to Santa, too," the boy griped.

"What do you mean?" Donovan asked, his eyebrows raised.

"You said he would find us wherever we were on Christmas, and he'd take our gifts there," Q reminded him.

"You did get a gift at Grandma's," Donovan noted.

"Yeah, but that wasn't from Santa. That was from Grandma."

"Maybe Santa forgot what house you were at," Kyra offered. "It's a simple mistake."

"So does that mean he didn't give us anything?"

Q was on the verge of a holiday breakdown. Donovan saw that Kat looked disappointed as well.

"Don't worry," Kyra told them. "Santa always finds a way."

Quinell had no choice but to accept that response until they got home. He was quiet and contemplative for the rest of the way. When they pulled into their driveway, he and Donovan brought the luggage in while Kyra helped Kat out of her car seat.

Upon entering their home, Quinell stopped short and stared at their Christmas tree with wide, unbelieving eyes. The handle of the suitcase he was carrying slipped from his limp hand. Grandma had brought him home last night, so he could feed and play with the dogs out back. There wasn't one single gift under the tree then, but now there were dozens. They were all wrapped with bright, colorful paper with pretty bows and ribbons.

Quinell approached the tree on noodle legs that threatened to give out with each step. He couldn't articulate a suitable comment for what he was seeing. Donovan followed him inside and appeared to be as shocked as he was.

"How?" Quinell asked. "What... how?"

"Would you look at that," Donovan said. "Looks like he found us after all."

"*Presents*!" Katavia screamed when she rushed in behind them. "Look, Mama! *Presents*! Santa came! *Santa came!*"

Q was torn between believing what he was seeing and what he knew to be real. Either way, the smile that spread across his face was as delightful as his grandmother's when Donovan delivered the news about Kyra's pregnancy.

"How did this happen?" Q asked as he dropped to his knees before the huge pile of gifts. "I was here last night. None of this was here." He looked back at Kyra. "Mama, is Santa Claus really real?"

"If not, we need to call the police," she told him, "'cause *somebody's* been up in our house!"

With that, the boy laughed and got down to the serious business of opening his gifts.

Donovan took a seat on the couch. Kyra sat next to him. He put his arm around her and she laid her head on his shoulder. They were full and tired and content and excited, all at the same time. Donovan reached to caress her belly. Kyra wasn't showing at all, but he knew what was going on in there, and it meant the world to him.

She placed her hand over his and smiled softly as they watched their children tear the wrapping paper off their gifts. Donovan wished he could stay in that moment forever, but he also looked forward to the days, weeks and years ahead.

"I think I'll take a nap after this," he told his wife.

"You deserve it," Kyra said. "But don't forget to open your gifts first."

"Oh, I won't. I can't wait to see what Santa got me."

"It's right here!" Q shouted, holding up a beautifully wrapped box. "Donovan, here's one of your presents!"

Despite his fatigue, Donovan had a pep in his step as he joined his children under the Christmas tree.

"Let me see what you got there, son…"

KEITH THOMAS WALKER

Author's Note: Thank you so much for your support! I hope you enjoyed Donovan and Kyra's story. Please continue reading Primal Part One (Primal is *erotica*)…

CHAPTER ONE
THE MIXER

Monica Wyatt sat at a table for four in a conference room at the downtown Hilton. She considered all of the other places she'd rather be as she made small talk with the ladies at her table. Across from her sat Jennifer Wheatfield. To her right was Veronica Mitchell, and to her left was Phyllis Millsap. Monica hadn't seen any of them since graduating high school, but she kept up with Veronica from time to time on Facebook.

The glorious event that brought the women together (as well as seventeen other members of their graduating class), was the *Finley High Class of '95 Mixer*. It was promoted as a smaller version of an official class reunion, which was probably due to the lack of interest the class of 1995 had in reuniting, even if only for one night.

But what was the point of seeing these people again? Who goes to high school reunions anyway? From the looks of it, not many. Monica hated high school, all the way up to her senior year. Her adolescence was tragically awkward. She remembered sucking in sports, surprise menstrual cycles, several broken hearts and mean girl cliques that kept her relegated to the outskirts of popular events.

The idea of a reunion meant she would want to *reunite* with the same people who alienated her at a time when she sought acceptance the most.

So why did she come?

Monica imagined she was there for the same reason everyone else had come: She wanted to see if the head cheerleader had gotten fat, if their valedictorian had become a rocket scientist and if any of their schoolyard bullies had gotten what they deserved in life; which would preferably be incarceration or one of those long, dark dirt naps. Sure, that was morbid, but Monica didn't think she was wrong or alone in this line of thinking.

But instead of determining whether her former classmates got their comeuppance, the Finley High mixer proved to be as big a bust as Mrs. Hodges' *Let's have class outside for the rest of the year* initiative in '94. That little project sent Peter Wessel to the ER with anaphylactic shock after Javier Nunez found a wasp nest and a poking stick and put two and two together.

Monica grinned at the memory. Peter's face had swelled to the size of a pumpkin, while Mrs. Hodges completely freaked out. If she had any emergency training, she forgot about it that day.

Good times.

It would've been nice to bring up that incident at Monica's table of four, but neither Peter nor Javier nor Mrs. Hodges attended the mixer. No one else in the conference room was in her history class that semester, so Monica sighed and forgot about the wasps and continued to nurse a Long Island iced tea – which was one of the few positive things she could say about this event: The drinks were free, and the bartender didn't skimp on the alcohol. Monica had been at the hotel for nearly an hour. She would've left thirty minutes ago if not for the bar, which she'd already visited twice.

The conference room was decorated with blue and white streamers, banners and posters; all reminiscent of what students might find hanging in the halls of Finley High before a pep rally. The DJ busied himself spinning tunes from the early nineties. The women at Monica's table were mostly quiet, but as the liquor coursed through their veins, they became a little more eager to speak on the failure of their twenty-year reunion.

"I thought more people would show up," Jennifer commented. She was a mousy woman with rosy cheeks and small teeth that didn't fit her face well.

"That's what I'm saying," Monica agreed as she looked around the mostly empty room. "Weren't you on the organizing committee?" she asked Veronica.

"I was," Veronica confirmed. She hadn't changed much since high school, except for an extra thirty pounds that was distributed nicely around her body. "It was me and Hasan. But we weren't getting much interest early on. That's why we decided to have a *mixer*, instead of a full-fledged reunion."

"I got the invite on Facebook," Phyllis said. "I started not to come, since I saw that only about twenty people had confirmed it."

"It's not that bad, is it?" Veronica asked. She looked as if the event was a personal failure on her part.

"The drinks are good," Monica said.

"Oh yeah, these are definitely worth it," Phyllis agreed. She downed the rest of a fruity concoction and placed her glass on the table. "I'll be here till midnight, as long as y'all keep serving free liquor."

The ladies laughed at that.

"They should be serving dinner soon," Veronica informed them. "I'm sure things will liven up after that."

Monica doubted that. Most of her former classmates seemed to be just as shy as they were in school. The boys didn't want to approach the females, the Asians were all sitting together, and no one wanted to raise their voice above the sound of the music. It was high school all over again! The only difference now was no one was anxious to graduate and take the world by storm. They tried that already, and their dreams had been crushed by the establishment. Now they were simply living check-to-check lifestyles, like their parents and grandparents had done before them.

"Well, what have you all been up to?" Veronica asked the women at her table. "We don't need three hundred people here to catch up with each other. Most of the ones who didn't show up were assholes anyway..."

The ladies agreed that was true, and they did have a good time trading stories with each other. A few minutes later the servers began to deliver their meals, which further helped to brighten their moods.

After dinner the guests began to move about a bit more. The DJ couldn't entice anyone to dance, but the former classmates were talkative and laughter could be heard from all corners of the room.

Monica was about to start offering her goodbyes when one of the ladies at her table grabbed her arm (rather roughly). With her free hand, she pointed at the entrance of the conference room.

"Ooh! *Ooh*!"

Monica turned and stared at her with a perplexed expression. It took Phyllis a few moments to get her words together.

"Look!" she said. "Isn't that *Jovan*? That's him! *That's Jovan*!"

Monica's face flushed with heat as she followed Phyllis' gaze and saw that Jovan Crist, one of few ex-boyfriends who actually *didn't* break her heart in high school, had indeed entered the room. In addition to heated, Monica wasn't sure why she suddenly felt unsure of herself and short of breath. It probably had a lot to do with the fact that Jovan had aged better than fine wine. It only took a brief glance to see that he still carried himself with the air of a king amongst peasants.

"Holy shit," Veronica muttered. Everyone at their table was watching him now, the whole room was. "He's fine as hell."

"For real," Phyllis agreed with a slow shake of her head. "Girl, I know you mad for letting that one get away. Do you still keep up with him?"

Monica frowned as she pulled her arm away – not that Phyllis noticed. Her eyes were glued on the mixer's new main attraction. Monica didn't think she would've gotten much of a reaction if she slapped the woman in the face, which, coincidentally, was something she felt like doing.

How did she let Jovan get away? What the hell kind of question was that? She dated the boy when they were *eighteen*. Did this bitch expect them to grow up and get married? What was the percentage of high school sweethearts who did that? And it wasn't like she and Jovan were *head-over-hills* at any point. They never even had sex.

Monica thought Phyllis' question was out of line. Or maybe she was taking it too seriously. That's what people did at reunions, right? They ask a bunch of stupid questions that don't mean shit because they're not shit, and they don't have shit going on!

Monica shook her head and tried to let go of an unexpected fit of anger. She wasn't sure where it had come from.

"No, I don't keep up with him," she replied to Phyllis. "I haven't seen the boy since we graduated."

"Really?" Veronica asked. "I thought you two were a great couple. I just knew you'd stay friends after graduation."

The ladies at the table continued to watch Jovan as he greeted old classmates; offering handshakes, brief hugs and a megawatt smile that he definitely improved upon since graduation. He wore dark pants with a tan shirt that went well with his golden brown skin. The shirt was short-sleeved, exposing powerful arm muscles that weren't there twenty years ago. He had his shirt unbuttoned nearly halfway down, which was obviously to flaunt his huge pectorals. Those muscles weren't fully developed in high school, either.

Jovan had a short afro when he and Monica dated. It didn't look like he'd cut his hair at all in twenty years. Tonight he had it styled in thin dreadlocks that were tied back behind his head. His features were a lot stronger than Monica remembered. His jaw line was definitely more rigid, his eyes more serious.

But there was no doubt this was the same boy she made out with in gym class and almost gave her virginity to in the twelfth grade. His smile revealed an innocence that hadn't changed over the years – despite the fact that everything below his smile was the exact opposite of innocent. Monica had to say her high school sweetheart looked downright sinful.

"He didn't have all those muscles in school," Phyllis noticed. She was practically drooling over him, which pissed Monica off even more.

"No, he was skinny," Jennifer agreed. "I don't know where he got all *that* from!"

"Did y'all ever have sex?" Phyllis asked, looking Monica's way again.

Monica couldn't believe this heifer's gall. She and Phyllis weren't friends in high school. In fact, Phyllis hung out with a group of pretty girls who did everything they could to make *normal* people like Monica feel marginalized. If Monica had been raised just a little bit differently, she would have brought a can of whoop-ass to this mixer and popped it open for bitches like Phyllis. That ass-whooping was two decades in the making.

But Monica never was one to fight, so she stood instead and told the women at the table, "Y'all are too much," before she headed for the bar. One more drink and she was out of there. She would've left without it, but she didn't want anyone to think it was Jovan's presence that drove her from the building.

CHAPTER TWO
JOVAN

After retrieving her spirits from the bartender, Monica scanned the room again, looking for a different table to park at. She didn't think she was avoiding Jovan, but there was no other way to explain a second bout of uneasiness that overcame her when she saw the man of the hour headed her way. Monica wasn't able to come to terms with her feelings before he was within a few feet; flashing a perfect smile that looked a whole lot less innocent as he drew near.

"*Monica Wyatt*! I'm so happy to see you!"

His voice was manly in high school. It was now a few octaves deeper. Monica didn't have a chance to respond before he closed the distance between them and hugged her tightly. She had seen him hug a few other women when he first arrived, and theirs was certainly not the same. This was no granny hug; with their hips far apart, as if there was an imaginary yard stick between their genitals. He hugged her fully, with both arms, belly to belly. Monica didn't completely return the gesture, because she was holding her drink, but Jovan did enough hugging for the both of them.

She found his cologne enchanting. Beneath it, she caught a trace of his natural musk, which was just as pleasant. Jovan's body was hard, but overall the hug was soft and warm. When he backed away, Monica found herself heated to the point of sweating. She prayed that wouldn't actually happen.

What the hell is wrong with you, woman?

She didn't have an answer for the voice in her head. She hoped she was reacting to the *new* Jovan, rather than any lingering feelings she might have had for the guy she once dated. She certainly hadn't been carrying a torch for the past twenty years, and she knew he hadn't either.

"It's good to see you, too," she told him. Her smile was bright and wide; she couldn't help it.

He released her but didn't step away more than arms' length. He continued to grin as he looked her up and down, taking in all of the things that had changed since high school.

Monica didn't dress that night with Jovan in mind, but she did dress to impress, considering it was a reunion. Her dress wasn't of the *freakum* variety, but it was short and form-fitting, exposing a nice amount of flesh about the chest and legs. Her skin tone was fair. Her shoulder-length hair was curly with gold highlights. She'd put on more than twenty pounds since graduation but was happy to say most of it went to the right places. Her breasts and thighs were fuller than Jovan recalled. Her lips and eyes were the same, though her face had a more mature look.

"Where'd you get that dress?" he asked, still smiling ear to ear. "I wish you would've dressed like this in high school! Naw, I take that back. I would've been so busy chasing you, I probably wouldn't have graduated." He laughed.

Monica giggled, though she was taken aback by his forwardness. Jovan had always been a pretty boy. He wasn't a full-fledged *player* at Finley High, but he certainly had player tendencies. She thought his confidence was level ten when they were going out. If that was the case, he was now up to level fifty.

"Whatever," she said. "And what have you been doing with yourself, Jovan, trying out for Mr. Universe?"

He laughed again. Monica loved the way his eyes twinkled when he was amused. His teeth were perfect. She loved a man with a sense of humor.

"I'm not that big," he said. "I work out a little bit, but I've been slacking."

"A little bit? Yeah, right. You don't get a body like that from working out *a little bit*. And look at your hair! I think it's longer than mine."

He grinned. She could tell he liked that she was checking him out.

"Hold on a sec'," he said and took a few steps to the bar.

Monica had a minute to pull herself together before he returned with Cognac on the rocks. The liquor matched his eyes and his skin tone. Monica saw that most of the women in the room were watching them – especially the ladies at the table she left a few minutes ago. She wondered what they expected to happen.

"So, what's been up with you?" Jovan asked as he sipped his drink. "I can't believe it's been twenty years since we graduated. You married yet? Kids?"

"I'm divorced," Monica said. "I have a daughter."

"Really? How old?"

"She's six."

"I'll bet she's beautiful," he said, "just like her mama."

Her heart fluttered. She felt the perspiration on her face and palms this time. "Boy, stop."

"No, I'm serious. You've gotten a lot finer since high school. If I would've known, I would've kept tabs on you."

She wondered what he meant by that. Their relationship didn't end badly, not that she recalled. It simply ran its course, and they moved on. She had no idea he would morph into this *earth-bound god*, but that didn't mean anything.

She doubted if he really thought she was that beautiful. He was probably just looking for a hookup for the night, in which case he was barking up the wrong tree. Monica wasn't going for it.

"You're not married?" she asked, looking at his hands. There was no wedding ring. "Any children of your own?"

He shook his head and took another sip of his drink. "Nope, on both counts."

"That's not surprising," she said with a slight roll of her eyes.

"Why you say that?"

"You don't look like the type to settle down."

He grinned. "What are you basing that on, Monica?"

The way he said her name made her stomach tighten. "The, the way you're dressed," she managed.

"Still not sure what you mean," he commented. "I just got on pants and a shirt, like anybody else." She thought his smile was predatory now.

"You got your shirt unbuttoned," she pointed out, "showing off your chest. You got the long hair, pretty eyes, muscles for days…"

He chuckled. "You think I look nice?"

"I think *you* think you look nice," she replied. "You know how to turn heads."

"Come on, Monica, you know me."

The way Jovan said her name, and the way he was watching her, seemed more intimate than everyone else she spoke to that night. It was almost enough to make her want to buy whatever it was he was selling. Almost.

"I don't know you like that," she replied. "I have no idea what you've been up to in the past twenty years."

He downed the rest of his drink with barely a reaction to the strong intoxicant.

"A little of this, a little of that," he said vaguely. "What about you? What kind of work you doing? You seeing anyone?"

Monica didn't know why he was asking about her relationship status. She already decided she wouldn't be his easy lay for the night, so she told him the same thing she had told the ladies at her table: "I've been seeing a guy for a little over a year. We work together sometimes."

If Jovan was disappointed by that news, it didn't show. "What kind of work do you do?"

"I'm a manager – and a club promoter."

His eyes lit up. He may have been faking his way through the conversation, but at that moment he was genuinely intrigued.

"Really? What kind of folks do you manage?"

"A few local acts," she said. "A couple of rappers... a singer."

"No shit? Hold on for a second."

He turned and took a few quick steps to the bar. While he was busy with another drink order, Monica scanned the room and saw that all eyes were on her – well,

Jovan to be specific. She was struck with an uncomfortable sense of déjà vu, remembering how it was for them in high school. Jovan was one of the most popular students on campus. A lot of chicks were campaigning to be his girlfriend. Most of them were not happy when he chose Monica for the coveted role.

They didn't try anything mean or underhanded to break them up, but they were always watching and lurking in the shadows. She knew they were waiting for her to screw up so they could jump in and *comfort* him – most likely with a sorry-for-the-break-up-blow job. Initially Monica felt special for being Jovan's girl. He could've picked anyone at the school, but his eyes only lit up for her. When they walked the hallways hand-in-hand, she was on cloud nine.

But over time the hate and animosity she got from her classmates got to be too much of a hindrance. Monica couldn't ignore the girls rolling their eyes every time she passed. She didn't like them eyeballing her boyfriend and flirting with him when she wasn't around. Even at the age of eighteen, it was clear that Jovan was a rock star. He already had a throng of groupies.

Monica couldn't be like them, and she didn't want to compete with them, so she chose to step aside and let him shine without her. When she told him she was through, Jovan didn't put up a fight to change her mind, which, as far as Monica was concerned, meant he never really loved her to begin with.

When he returned with his drink, she was ready to bid him adieu and once again leave him to his groupies. But Jovan was hoping to keep her around for a while longer. In addition to his glass, he had one for her as well.

"I asked the bartender what you were drinking," he said as he offered it to her. "I was hoping we could sit and talk for a minute."

She took the drink but told him, "No, actually I was about to take off."

"Really?" He looked upset by that. "But I just got here."

"Yeah, over an hour late," she commented. "We already had dinner and everything."

"Can't you stay longer, so we can talk?"

Monica shook her head. *Nope. Not tonight, Mr. Smooth.* "About what?" she asked.

He surprised her with, "About your job. I was watching this show on cable; *Power*. Do club promoters really do all that crazy shit to make sure they stay packed?"

Monica frowned. She didn't think anyone had ever asked her that. "We do," she confirmed, "but not like on TV. Anything you've seen on that show is way more interesting than what I do."

"What's the weirdest thing you've done for your club?" he pressed. "Anything *illegal*?"

Her frown deepened. She didn't like this line of questioning. "Why are you asking me that?"

He laughed. Again Monica was struck by how beautiful his smile was. His teeth were straight and gleaming. Women had been fighting over that smile for years, hoping it would be directed at them.

"Why you being so standoffish?" he wondered. "You're acting like we're not friends."

"We're not friends. I haven't seen you in twenty years."

"But nothing happened to make you *not* be my friend. We didn't fall out, or anything."

"Okay, but why are you asking about my job? You need a promoter, or something?"

He continued to smile over his glass as he took a sip. He nodded slightly. "A promoter, manager... Yeah, that would be great. You taking new clients?"

Monica wasn't sure if she could take him seriously. "And what is it that you do, Jovan?"

"Jovan?"

They both turned to acknowledge one of his groupies. Her name was Amanda. Monica wasn't positive, but she thought Jovan went out with her his junior year. Unlike most of the black guys in their graduating class, Jovan was an equal opportunity employer.

White, black, Puerto Rican, everybody just-a-freaking!

"Hey, girl! Look at you!"

He threw his arms around Amanda for one of the full-body hugs that made Monica feel special a few minutes ago.

Some things never change, she thought as she backed away and gave them some space.

• • • • • •

By 10:30 the moon was on the rise in the starry skies above Overbrook Meadows. The night air was warm and still. Monica fished her car keys from her purse as she approached her Yukon in the hotel's parking lot. She thought she had escaped the mixer unnoticed, but she heard a second set of footsteps accompanying hers. They were closing in, moving quickly. She turned, hoping she wasn't about to get mugged, and was surprised to see Jovan hurrying to catch up with her.

He was not a welcomed sight, but the look of irritation she wore as he approached was unintentional. He stopped short ten feet away and regarded her curiously.

"Wow. What in the world is your problem?"

The emotions Monica had been feeling since she saw him swept her up in a whirlwind. She had plenty of answers to his question, but her lips remained sealed. The fact of the matter was Jovan made her feel like she wasn't good enough – for him or life in general – and she hadn't felt that way in a long time. She didn't like how he reentered her world and took her right back to her awkward, confusing high school experience. She didn't feel like that before he arrived tonight. It was definitely him.

Why the hell did she come to this mixer? This was probably why only a few people bothered to show up. High school was bad enough the first time around. No one wanted to experience it again, even in little doses.

She sighed and tried to look nonchalant. "Sorry. It's – nothing. I'm fine."

"Why'd you take off?" he asked and took a few guarded steps in her direction.

"You were a little busy in there," she informed him. "I didn't think you'd notice."

He grinned and reached to rub the hair on the top of his head. He stroked it backwards, towards the rubber band that held his dreads together. His biceps were huge. His triceps were too. His forearm looked strong enough to crack a skull.

"I know you not getting jealous," he said. "You said you got a man."

"I'm not jealous," Monica said, frowning again. "Why would I be jealous? I don't even know you – not like that."

"I have to be available to women," he explained. "It's business, or it could be. You never know."

"What the hell does that mean?" In addition to being insanely sexy, Jovan was a walking question mark.

"Where you headed?" he asked. "Can we go somewhere and talk?"

"I gotta go to work," she said, blowing him off.

"Where do you work, that you have to be there at eleven o'clock at night."

"One of my clients has a gig," she explained. "On the weekends I work as late as three in the morning." She wasn't sure why she felt compelled to explain herself.

"What club?" he asked. "Can I go? I'll meet you there."

"Why do you wanna talk to me?" she asked, growing exasperated. "I already told you ain't nothing happening between us."

His mouth fell open. He closed it and smiled good-naturedly. "Monica, I respect your relationship. Trust me. I want to talk about *business*," he insisted. He was as calm as she was agitated. "How much are you making off your client tonight?" Before she could respond, he said, "I know it's not as much as you can get working with me."

Monica stared at him with her mouth ajar, eyes unblinking. "How do you know that? You still haven't told me what you do, Jovan. Sing, dance? You a stripper?"

He shrugged. "I do a lot of stuff. Does that mean you wanna talk business?"

She didn't, but then again maybe she did. The singer she was managing tonight, Shayne, was only getting $750 for his performance. Monica's 20 percent take was a whopping 150 bucks. Jovan had no way of knowing any of that. But his boast that she could make more money working with him got her attention.

"I'll be at Club Tron," she told him before opening the door and slipping inside her car.

Jovan stood watching and smiling until she rolled out of the parking lot.

CHAPTER THREE
NOT REALLY MODELING

Club Tron was a staple on the city's south side. The modest establishment offered a competitive ladies' night on Fridays and was home to MC Freeze; arguably one of the top five DJs in the area. The club wasn't in a great neighborhood and didn't attract the right crowd to bring in any serious talent, but they managed to book a live performer each month. Tonight it was Shayne, an up and coming R&B singer from North Dallas.

Shayne had the looks and style to take him to the next level. He was tall and thin, with short hair and pretty eyes. His stage presence was another strong point. His vocal skills weren't where Monica wanted them to be, but he was young. She thought he was getting better with each performance.

By 12:30 his show was in full swing. The club was filled with tipsy, scantily clad women. A good number of them stood at the front of the stage, screaming and vying for the singer's attention. Monica made sure to get them in the photos and videos she uploaded to Shayne's Twitter and Instagram accounts.

In addition to being his manager and stylist, she was a ceaseless promoter for Shayne and all of her other clients. So far none of them had become the next Drake or Trey Songz, but Monica remained hopeful. She never knew which new contact would be the one to change her client's life and hers as well. She was sure it was only a matter of time.

She was aware of Jovan as soon as he entered the club, though he didn't immediately seek her out or give any outward indication that he was there for her. He breezed into the building with confidence and familiarity, as if he patronized the nightclub on a regular basis. Monica knew that was not the case, because Club Tron was another one of her clients. She was there almost every weekend, and she had never seen him.

Her ex-boyfriend stood out in the crowd, not only because of his massive size, but because of his dress. Jovan was GQ smooth amongst a crowd of hustlers and roughnecks. Dozens of eyes were on him as he acclimated himself to the environment and made his way to the bar. He offered the barkeep an easy smile. She was wrapped around his finger after a few exchanges. Jovan struck up a conversation with another woman seated next to him before stepping away with his drink. It looked like the same concoction he ordered at the mixer; Cognac on the rocks.

Monica lost track of him. She waited a while and then left her seat. She slowly made her way around the club, using the darkness and the crowd to conceal her. She spotted Jovan as he took a seat at an empty table. His attention was focused on the stage, where Shayne was crooning to a beautiful sister in a little red dress. Shayne was doing a great job. Monica was not in position to photograph her client's latest move.

After a few minutes, she moved again; this time to a table that was occupied by two men.

"Mind if I sit here for a second?"

They looked her up and down. Pretty, fair skin, short in stature, big boobs and thick thighs... They didn't mind at all.

Monica watched her high school crush for a while longer, long enough to see two women approach his table. They initiated the conversation. Jovan said something, and they were all smiles and giggles. He invited them to join him, and they did.

Monica was not surprised that he attracted so much attention, but she was startled by the ease in which he settled into the scene and wasted no time hooking up with a couple of cuties. The Jovan she knew in high school was handsome but *sweet*. She expected him to marry a beautiful woman and settle down – not turn into an arrogant ladies' man.

Or maybe she was judging him too harshly. Monica wondered if it was green-eyed envy that had her turning up her nose at her old friend. She wasn't jealous because she wanted him back, rather it was Jovan's seemingly freestyle life that irked her. She knew it was wrong to formulate that opinion, because she had such little to go on. For all she knew he worked 80 hours a week and chose to have a little fun tonight.

She turned her back on Jovan and returned to her original seat.

• • • • • •

He approached her an hour later. Shayne was done performing by then. He was chilling in the VIP with two of his personal friends and four women they met that night. Monica thought her client had the air of a superstar. She hoped someone important would agree with her soon, a record executive would be nice.

Jovan said, "Great show. Is that one of the guy's you're managing?" He placed two drinks on the table.

Monica noticed that he remembered what she was drinking at the mixer. She smiled as she took her glass. "Yes. Did you like him?"

"He's... not bad." Jovan took a seat across from her. "He has a nice look. Are you his stylist?"

Monica's eyes narrowed. Her smile remained. "Yes. Sometimes. You like his outfit?"

He nodded, looking into her eyes. "I do."

Monica felt a sudden chill, which she attributed to the strength of his gaze. It's not every day that someone so attractive looks directly at you, sitting so closely. Jovan used to make her feel that way in high school, but he was different now, more virile.

"How much of the show did you catch?" She knew the answer to that and was curious about whether he'd be honest.

"I've been here about an hour."

Okay, so he told the truth. But why did he wait so long to come to her table, if he came to see her?

Around them club-goers moved about casually as MC Freeze transitioned into a Chris Brown mix. A few ladies sent smiles Jovan's way as they passed, even though he was seated with another woman. He vaguely returned their attention, which Monica was okay with. It wasn't like they were on a date. This was supposed to be a business meeting, and she was eager to get on with it.

"So, you had something you'd like to discuss?"

Jovan nodded, his attention solely on her now. "Yes." He leaned closer. "I think we might be able to work together on a project of mine."

"What kind of project?"

"What's been going on with you since we graduated?" he asked. "When we were going out, you talked about going to OSU..."

She wanted to keep their conversation on track, but there was no need to be rude. They were once good friends, and she hadn't seen him in a very long time. Catching up was in order.

"I did. I majored in business management. But I didn't finish."

"Me neither!"

Monica wasn't sure why he was so excited about that.

"What'd you major in?" she asked.

He shrugged. "I was still working on my basics."

She shook her head, grinning. "Well, at least I made it to my junior year."

"Why'd you quit?"

"I got a job offer. It was the job I thought I needed college for. You know how it is when you're in your twenties; always looking for an easy route."

"Oh, I know all about that," he agreed. "But that's not just a twenties' feeling. I'm still doing it in my thirties. Nothing wrong with the easy route. What was the job that took you out of school?"

"I got an offer to manage three Luby's."

"*Luby's*? Do they even have those anymore?"

She laughed softly. "I'm sure they're still around."

"Managing three restaurants when you're 21," he mused. "The owner must've thought very highly of you."

"We were dating for a little bit." She wasn't sure why she chose to reveal that.

Jovan chuckled. He grinned at her. "How'd you go from Luby's to R&B singers?"

"There was a lot in between. I got tired of having to be on someone else's schedule all the time. Owning your own business... That's the American dream, right?"

He nodded. "Yes. I know exactly how you feel."

After a pause, she asked, "What about you? What have you been up to since Finley High, besides growing all that hair?"

He smiled and thought for a moment. "A lot."

Monica's lips curved into a grin. "Yeah, I guessed that." She waited, thinking he'd elaborate. Instead he redirected the conversation back to her.

"How's business going? Do you have a lot of clients?"

Monica felt like any number less than 100 would make her sound like a failure. "I have six, and I do promotions for two clubs."

He lifted his glass and sipped slowly. She couldn't tell if he was impressed.

He said, "That's a lot. You must be living well."

She was guarded now. "I do okay. But I'm not ready for retirement."

"Do you have assistants?"

She shook her head slowly. Her cousin Jeanette helped out a little, but she couldn't consider it full or even part-time employment. "Nope. Just me. I'm hoping to expand. I've only been doing this for a few years. Why are you asking?"

"I'm thinking about hiring you. I knew there was a reason I went to that whack-ass mixer. I think you're it." His smile was delicious.

Monica was flattered, but her suspicion remained. "Hiring me for what, Jovan? What kind of work do you do?"

He continued to grin at her. "Modeling."

She sighed inwardly. Of course a perfectly sculpted pretty-boy wanted someone to take pictures of him. She shook her head. "I don't manage models."

If he was disappointed, he hid it well. "Why not?"

"I don't know enough about the modeling business. I don't know *anything* about the modeling business."

"I could teach you."

Monica had a tempting vision of them working closely together as he *taught* her. "Do you model, like, full-time? It's your only job?" She couldn't believe she was considering it.

He nodded.

She studied him closely. He was clean-shaven. His eyebrows were arched perfectly. Those eyebrows were just as perfect when he was 18, so she didn't think he got them sculpted. But now that she knew he was a model, maybe he did.

She thought his outfit was perfect, in style and fit. His dreads were neat. Tonight they were tied back, but Jovan could create a few different looks if he let them down. He'd look good in anything, from Fendi suits to basketball gear. He looked powerful, sexy and intelligent. Throw a pair of shades on him, and he could be a gangster or a hit man. Monica couldn't deny that she was eager to see more of him.

"Do you have a portfolio?"

She knew he wasn't carrying anything, so she expected him to tell her where she could find it online. But Jovan shook his head.

"I don't really model anymore."

Monica continued to stare at him, rather than point out what little sense he was making.

He laughed. "I know you're gonna think this is weird. *Shocking*, even. But if you hear me out and keep an open mind, I think we could make a lot of money. I have the talent. But I need someone to put everything together; keep it straight and keep it growing; keep me out of trouble."

Monica didn't know what to think. Money was always a driving force, but his comments revealed a lot of pitfalls. *Weird*? *Shocking*? Whatever he was into was probably illegal.

She already knew she wasn't interested when she asked, "What the hell do you do, Jovan?"

"It's a... dating service."

"*Dating*?" The hairs on the back of her neck stiffened. "Like escorts?"

He nodded. "Yeah, like escorts..."

"You're a–" Her face reddened. She leaned over the table and hissed, "*male prostitute*?"

"Whoa." Jovan held up two perfectly manicured hands. "That's such an ugly word."

Monica's jaw remained unhinged while she waited for him to deny the charge. But he didn't.

CHAPTER FOUR
GIGOLO

> *Licking, sucking, fucking*
> *Pay me*
> *You dripping*
> *I sop it up like gravy*
> *Pay me*
> *Foaming at the mouth*
> *Like I got rabies*
> *Pay me*
> *We can make love*
> *Not babies*
> *Pay me*
> *Smack it up, flip it, touch it*
> *Pay me*
> *I'm licking, I'm sucking, I'm fucking*
> *Pay me*

She wasn't sure how long she sat there staring at him. Despite the serious look in his eyes, he was smiling, so she held out hope that he was kidding. An escort? Jovan? As outgoing as he'd always been, she couldn't imagine him taking that route. Sex for money? No, not him.

She thought back to their sexual relationship, which was nonexistent – thankfully. Or maybe she had slighted herself by not giving in to temptation when they were teens. Was Jovan *that* good in bed? Good enough to charge for it? This was surreal. But as the seconds ticked on, and Monica began to blink and breathe again, he didn't tell her this was all a ruse; a silly joke he played on long lost friends.

"You're serious aren't you?"

He nodded. "I haven't been doing it that long."

"How... *Why*?" She shook her head in exasperation. "How did this happen."

He laughed. Monica became more aware of his perfectly straight teeth, his strong jaw line, his Adam's apple. How many women had kissed those lips? Where had life taken the boy she dated for the first four months of their senior year? Jovan took her to Finley High's homecoming game. They made out long and hard that night, but she never reached into his lap, and he didn't slip a hand inside her panties.

When he was done laughing, he asked, "Are you hungry? Wanna get something to eat?"

She did, but she didn't know if she wanted to hang out with the likes of him. She chuckled, catching herself. The club business was filled with shady characters. She knew a lot of drug dealers. She brought in a few *women of ill repute* to keep the VIP happy on multiple occasions. But she never thought about managing them. What would that make her, a pimp?

This was too much.

"Are you gonna be okay?" he asked.

"Yeah," she said, struggling to get her thoughts together. "Sure."

"So, you wanna get something to eat?" he asked again. As she checked the time on her phone, he said, "There's an I HOP not too far from here."

As far as late night dining went, that wasn't a bad choice. It was better than the Waffle House, where club-hoppers loved to settle their late night beefs. But if she agreed to go with him, she would also be agreeing to entertain his indecent proposal.

She sighed and convinced herself there was nothing wrong with hearing him out. If anything, she had to know how a boy she went to school with got himself involved in the world's oldest profession.

"Alright," she told him. "I can meet you there in forty-five minutes. I have to take care of some things here first."

He smiled graciously. "Great. Me too! Your boyfriend will be okay with you being out so late?"

Monica forgot she had told him that. "Oh, yeah, he'll be fine. This is business, right?"

He nodded. "Of course. I'll see you there."

He stood and helped her to her feet. As she stepped away, she wondered about his *Me too*, comment. Did Jovan have business with someone at the club? There were a lot of eyes on him tonight. If one of the ladies he met wanted to hook up, how would he talk them into paying for it? Surely he wasn't that bold.

She couldn't have been more intrigued.

● ● ● ● ● ●

She arrived at the restaurant first. Before she got out of her car, she saw Jovan pull up in a pearl white BMW. The car looked to be no more than two years old. She met up with him as he exited the vehicle.

"Whatever you're doing seems to be paying well," she commented.

"Not whatever – *whoever*," he said and chirped the alarm.

It was after two a.m. when they were seated in a booth near the front of the restaurant. Jovan ordered waffles, while Monica opted for chicken Florentine crepes. While they waited for their food, she thought back to their first date in 1994. Jovan took her to a burger joint, which she considered fine dining at the time. He picked her up in a T-top Camaro. Monica's sister warned her that any boy who drove a car like that was sure to be moving way too fast for her, but that wasn't the case with Jovan.

He was smart, witty and funny. Monica didn't run him off when she wouldn't kiss on the first date or when she wouldn't have sex after the fifth. Jovan said he liked that she was different, and he'd be respectful of her decision to wait – not that it stopped him from trying. There were many instances when their kissing and touching transitioned well past second base, but Monica would always catch herself.

As far as she could tell, Jovan was never resentful when he repositioned his boner, so it wouldn't bump the steering wheel as he drove her home. But then again, they did break up after only four months of dating. Monica knew that Jovan went on to enjoy several fruitful and sexual relationships after her.

By the time they graduated, he had solidified his role as one of the smoothest brothers to ever walk the halls of Finley High. Monica's accomplishment of being the one girl who *didn't* give it up to him was mostly forgotten.

Their food was delivered after a rather long wait. Jovan thanked their waitress and dove into the meal, as if he hadn't eaten anything all day.

"Damn," Monica commented. "Are you starving, or is it that good?"

He swallowed before saying, "Both. I didn't make it to the mixer in time for dinner, remember?"

"Yes. You were fashionably late – which worked out perfectly, because all eyes were on you when you got there."

He looked up from his plate and smiled. "Were they?"

"You made quite an entrance," Monica acknowledged. "The ladies at my table, you were all they cared about from the moment they saw you."

He chuckled at that.

Monica raised an eyebrow. "Don't tell me you're modest."

He shook his head. "No. It comes with the business. Getting women's attention is half the battle."

Monica cut into her crepes. "You mean the modeling business or your *other* business?"

"I don't really model anymore," he stated. "I mean my other business."

"Were you working tonight?" she wondered.

"I'm always working. Even if it's only to make contact with a potential client, it's working, flirting, whatever."

She shook her head, smirking, as she devoured a bit of her food. It was good, definitely worth the wait. She said, "I was wondering how you go about that. If you meet a woman who likes you, how do you break the news to her that you charge for..." She looked around to make sure no one was eavesdropping before she murmured the word, "*sex*?"

Jovan found her unease amusing. "It's not the easiest thing to do," he confessed. "It's a feeling process. If I get a sense they wouldn't be down for it, I won't tell them at all."

"And you won't go out with them?"

"Sometimes I will," he said. "I'm telling you, there's no set of rules that works for every woman. Maybe I can't tell her I'm an escort, but I *can* tell her I'm between jobs, and I need things; groceries, bill money, rent... But I'm hoping to streamline the process, to take the guess work out of it. I don't like to scout potential clients. I need them to come to me, with no pretense in mind. That's what I've been working on. That's what I need you for."

Monica was no longer shocked by what she was hearing, but every layer of Jovan's story was fascinating. She'd never met a full-time gigolo – or at least not one who was willing to admit it.

"Tell me how this started."

"It was a gradual process," Jovan said as he continued his dinner. "It took twenty years of loafing and debauchery to get to this point."

Monica laughed nervously. She couldn't take her eyes off him. "You didn't get a body like that from loafing..."

He shook his head, looking into her eyes. "No. I started working out real heavy when I got to Texas Lutheran. My mom paid for me to live in the dorms my freshman year. They paired me up with another freshman who was on the football team. He was from Louisiana. They gave him a full ride. He was always complaining about how much the team sucked. He thought I could make it as a redshirt, if I had any athletic skills at all."

Jovan chuckled at the memory. "I never made the team, but I hung around them long enough to get acquainted with the weight room. The guys in there, the regulars, they knew all kinds of tricks for bulking up fast. A dude named Shannon took me under his wing. He was a hardcore lifter; shooting 'roids and everything. I never got into that, but I did the vitamins, protein shakes and weight gainers.

"I put on twenty-five pounds by the end of my freshman year. *All muscle.* I got a girl named Allyson to buy my books the second semester, and I pocketed the money my mom sent me."

Monica thought his smile was conniving now, as he reflected.

"If I had to pick the woman who started it all for me, I guess it would be Allyson," he continued. "I don't know why she felt the need to pay for something she was already getting for free, but she did. She liked to give. After a while, I wanted to please her more and more, just to see how far she would go. Every time she came, I wondered how much that was worth to her. It got to the point where I didn't even care about getting mine. But she did. She would please me and pay me. It was the best thing in the world."

Monica's eyes were wide, partially due to the casual manner in which he reported this. She realized her mouth was open, and she snapped it closed.

"Sorry, is this too much for you?" he asked. Her embarrassment was cute.

"No. It's just, it's not every day that one of your ex-boyfriends gets into... your line of work. But go on. I wanna hear your story."

"So, you want the dirty details?" His eyes were sinful.

Monica didn't want to be the one to back down. "What do you think I'm gonna do, whip out a bible and demand that everyone in the restaurant take part in stoning you?"

He laughed at that. "You sure you won't judge me?"

"You didn't ask me out on a date," she reminded him. "This is business. I wouldn't be here if I wasn't willing to offer an open mind."

He nodded. "Alright. So after I learned how to suck Allyson's clit until it rained money…"

Monica assumed the pause was to assess her reaction to that. She didn't bat an eye.

"I'm just kidding." He snickered. "I'd be rich by now, if I figured it out way back then. Nah, I spent the past twenty years working, mostly legit. I've done all kinds of things to make ends meet."

"Like what?"

"Modeling. Customer service." He rubbed his chin, thinking back. "I was a personal trainer for a while. I was a salesman."

"What kind of salesman?"

"You name it. I've sold everything from cars to washing machines. I can be pretty persuasive, especially if my customer is female."

Monica didn't doubt that. If his looks didn't pull you in – which they would – you would be drawn to Jovan's vernacular, his sense of humor and his confidence. She wondered what sort of things he'd talk her into by the end of the night.

"I've basically been a swindler for a long time," he revealed. "I've been a gigolo since college."

She shook her head. "You like that word, *gigolo*?"

"Everything else sounds feminine," he replied. "I like gigolo. It's fitting."

"Okay."

"I haven't worked much in the past couple of years," he said. "I think I made twenty thousand last year – legally."

Monica knew he wasn't pimping a BMW with those earnings. "How much you making with your side project?"

He shrugged. "Honestly I don't know. That's part of the reason I need a manager. I want to retire one day. I need help strategizing. Lately my life has been pretty carefree. I'll admit it."

"Do you have another Allyson taking care of you?" she wondered.

He smiled broadly. His pride was unmistakable. "I have *several* Allysons."

Wow. "You changed a lot." She didn't mean to say that. She didn't want to sound judgmental.

He said, "You have too. You've grown into a beautiful, mature woman. It's great to see you again, talk to you."

She had to look away from his eyes. They were enchanting. She stared at his mane instead. His dreads were perfect, no new growth at all. And they were clean, which was not always a given for that hairstyle. She wanted to see what his hair looked like when he let it down.

"If your Allysons are taking such good care of you, why do you want to take it any further? Sounds like you got a good thing going."

"I went to Vegas."

She brought a hand up to smother her laughter.

His eyes twinkled. "I love to see you laugh. I miss that. I miss you."

Her face heated. "I miss you too, Jovan – even though you're a lot different now."

"I've changed for the better," he assured her.

"We'll see. Tell me what happened in Vegas."

He raised one eyebrow. It was a small, sexy gesture. "Now, you know they say: What happens in Vegas–"

"Bullshit. Don't get shy on me now."

He studied her soft features, wondering why she never gave it up in high school. Back then, Monica was not like the others. But if he'd given it his all...

He said, "I met a lot of prostitutes in Vegas. They were... inspirational."

CHAPTER FIVE
LIKE FATHER, LIKE SON

Flesh of my flesh
Bone of my bone
God gave me a rib
So why should I roam?
Why should I disappear
And not answer the phone
And forget I have children?
Like a dog with a bone
Sniffing for some new tail
Gotta have it
I'm gone

The trip to Vegas was to celebrate Morris Glover's upcoming nuptials. Jovan had known Morris since the sixth grade. They grew up in the same neighborhood and attended school together until Jovan graduated two years ahead of him. Jovan's younger brother Luke was Morris' age, so they were closer childhood friends. As adults the threesome was as thick as thieves. For the Vegas trip, Morris invited another homey, Jesse, who was a friend from work.

The guys gave Morris a hard time about willingly giving up his player card and agreeing to have sex with only one woman for the rest of his life, but it was all in good fun. Jovan knew Morris' fiancé personally, and he thought his buddy had made an excellent pick.

Vivian was smart and focused; a homicide detective for Overbrook Meadows PD. Not only could she cook a mean casserole, but she could hold her own in a room full of surly men. Plus she had given Morris two sweet, baby girls; one of which was about to start Pre-K. Stepping up to the plate and marrying her was not only Morris' best move, but it was long overdue.

But that didn't stop his buddies from giving him a hard time as they sat near the bar at the extravagant Palazzo Hotel. It was after midnight on a warm, moonlit night. The sights and sounds from the casino were electrifying. Morris' crew was liquored-up and boisterous. Friday was the first of two nights they'd be in town. They all looked forward to his official bachelor party on Saturday.

"Tell me you're gonna get some ass while we're down here," Luke said.

"Man, you tripping," Morris replied. He was a tall man with an okay build. Anyone who saw his gut could tell that he had a woman at home taking care of him.

"Naw, for real, though," Luke pressed. "We in Vegas now, where anything goes. It wouldn't even be considered cheating."

Jovan's brother was nearly as handsome as he was and almost as buff. When Jovan made weight training a priority in college, his little brother was his favorite and most reliable workout buddy. Luke was able to achieve a well-toned, muscular physique, but he was five inches shorter than Jovan and couldn't reach his brother's massive size. In his heyday, Jovan tipped the scale at 240 pounds of mostly hulkish muscles, while his brother felt more comfortable at 210.

"Just because we're in Vegas don't mean I got a green light to cheat," Morris told him. "Viv was cool enough to let me come. I don't wanna do anything to ruin it when I get back."

"Did she tell you specifically *not to* cheat?" Luke wondered.

Morris shook his head. "She told me not to do anything that would make it hard for me to look her in the eyes when I get back."

"Shit, sounds like a green light to me!" Luke laughed and reached for Jovan to cosign on that.

Jovan didn't agree, but he didn't want to leave his brother hanging. He gave him a high-five.

"Fuck that," Jesse stated. He took a swig of his beer and leaned back, shaking his head. "Viv has a closet full of guns. I wouldn't fuck around on her. Might end up catching something worse than an STD – and yeah, I'm talking about a *bullet*!"

Everyone at the table laughed at that, except Jovan. For him, the comment hit a little close to home.

"Well, I don't know about y'all, but I'm trying to get my dick wet before we head home," Luke reported.

That was news to his brother. "Man, get out of here," Jovan replied.

"Nah, for real." Luke was animated. "We in Vegas, baby! Everything's legal over here."

"It may be legal, but it won't save you from getting a divorce," Morris informed him. "I know Cathy didn't give your ass a green light. It's not even your bachelor party!"

"I don't need a green light," Luke told them. "I'm careful with mines." He rubbed his hands together. "The only way Cathy will find out what happened here is if one of *you* motherfuckers tells her. And I know I ain't hanging with no snitches."

Luke looked around the table, waiting for someone to contradict him. But his statement was correct. Jovan wouldn't rat on his brother, and Morris had been their friend for more than 25 years. He wouldn't break his confidence, either. The only person at the table Luke didn't know very well was Jesse. But that was fine, because Jesse didn't know his wife.

"Nigga, you tripping," Jovan said, as he always did when his brother spoke on his adulterous fantasies. Jovan loved his sister-in-law dearly. He never wanted to see Cathy's world ripped apart simply because his little brother wanted to take a dip in some *new-new*.

"Nah, man," Luke said. "I been wanting to get out here for a minute. *Legal prostitution.* I gotta see what that looks like."

Jovan's brow furrowed as he watched him. He hoped he would let it go, but it sounded like Luke was serious.

"You wanna see what legal prostitution looks like?" Morris asked. "Hell, man, just look around. It looks exactly like what you see. Damned near half the women in here are hookers."

Luke's eyes widened. "No shit?"

"The fine ones are," Morris told him. "Anybody you see under the age of thirty, showing off half their ass, is probably a hoe. If you got the cash, they'll follow you up to your room."

"Don't tell him that," Jovan said, but he was too late. Luke was looking around the room with wolfish eyes.

"You don't say…"

"Let's take a walk," Jovan suggested, rising to his feet. "We can look together."

"That's what I'm talking about," Luke said as he rose from his seat.

"We'll be back in a minute," Jovan told the others.

Morris shrugged. "Take your time. We're probably gonna check out the casino…"

●●●●●●

Jovan tried to hold his tongue as he and his brother strolled through the hotel lobby. For them, this was supposed to be a pleasant vacation. They were there to support and celebrate with Morris. Jovan didn't want to argue, but he felt he had to intervene before Luke made another boneheaded decision.

"You're not gonna cheat on Cathy while we're down here."

Luke took a break from looking for his next conquest and met his brother's eyes.

"Why it sound like you're giving me an order?"

"You're a grown man," Jovan stated. "I'm not giving you an order. This is sound advice."

"We're in the land of tits and ass, and you're telling me to keep my pants on?" He snorted. "But you get to have all the fun you want, huh?"

"I'm not the one who got married," Jovan reminded him. "You think the grass is greener on my side, but sometimes I think you got it better. You got three kids, man. You got a wife to wake up to and go to bed with at night. Ain't no bitch in this state worth losing all that."

"I don't wanna give up my life," Luke retorted. "Never said that. Why you gotta take it there? What's wrong with me getting some skins while we're here and continuing my so-called perfect life when we get home?"

Jovan shrugged. "Nothing. Dad thought it wasn't nothing wrong with it, either."

"Man, *goddamn*," Luke said with a sneer. "Why you gotta bring that shit up?"

"Jesse the one brought it up. He said Morris might catch a bullet, if Viv caught him fucking around."

"He was just talking, Jovan. But you're serious. I don't want you jinxing me."

Jovan had to laugh at that. "You think I'm jinxing you?"

"Yeah, man. That's like, I'm fixing to get in the car, and you say, '*I hope you don't get in a wreck and die.*' You don't do that shit. Ain't cool, man."

Jovan put an arm around his neck. "I don't wanna jinx you, bro. Just trying to keep you straight."

Luke continued to sulk, while Jovan wondered why he needed a reminder about their father. Lamar Crist was a good man, overall, but like anyone he had his share of flaws. Adultery was the one he struggled with the most, and it was also the cause of his death fifteen years ago.

After three years of living as his side-chick, Lamar's mistress suffered a great bout of depression. Lamar didn't realize how far she'd declined mentally until it was too late.

She shot him while he slept and then turned the gun on herself. Jovan's mother didn't know about the affair until the police gave her the grisly details.

After losing their father in such a cruel manner and watching their mother cope with the betrayal, Jovan developed a renewed respect for the holiest of unions. He thought his brother was on the same page, but less than two years after Luke's marriage, his eyes began to wander.

Jovan wished he could say his brother was merely window-shopping, but he knew Luke had taken the full plunge more than a few times. Thankfully, Cathy was still unaware of his infidelities.

"Hey, boys! Y'all looking for some company?"

They turned and saw two voluptuous vixens standing shoulder to shoulder; one white, one black. Jovan thought the white girl was cuter, while her friend had a better figure. Either way, they couldn't have showed up at a worse time.

"Shit, hell yeah!" Luke's smile was ear to ear, his eyes as big as quarters.

He was a tall man with light brown skin, strong facial features and a remarkable resemblance to his big brother. Luke chose to keep his hair cut short, whereas Jovan wore his long.

"What are y'all getting into?" the blonde asked. She wore a halter top and mini-skirt. The only thing missing was a sash across her chest with the word "**HOOKER**" printed on it.

"Y'all got a room here?" her ebony friend inquired. She was dressed more conservatively in black, stretch pants, but her occupational status was clear as well. She had enough cleavage exposed to lose a whole wallet in it.

Jovan thought they were both delectable, but chocolate had always been his favorite.

"Yeah, we got a room upstairs," Luke announced. "Y'all wanna see it?"

Jovan chuckled inwardly. He knew where this was going, but Luke seemed oblivious.

"Yeah, we wanna go with you, daddy," the black girl said. "You want both of us, or you wanna pick?"

Luke couldn't stop himself from salivating. He had hit the jackpot.

"Man, both of y'all can come! We can have a party."

The girls smiled flirtatiously, and then the blonde dropped the bomb. "You can have us all night for two thousand."

Luke's eyes grew even larger, while Jovan stifled a chuckle.

"*Two thousand*? Are you serious?"

"It'll be half that, if you just want me," the black girl said.

"Or just me," her friend threw in.

Neither of them looked disappointed about Luke's initial reaction.

"A thousand dollars?" he scoffed. "That's crazy."

"I can spend an hour with you for five hundred," the blonde offered.

"Me, too," her friend said.

Luke continued to shake his head. "Nah, that's alright. I think we'll keep looking."

"You're not gonna find anything better," the black girl scoffed. "Come find us when you change your mind."

They turned, and the men stared at their asses as they walked away.

"*A thousand dollars*," Luke grumbled when they got moving again. "You knew they charged that much?"

"I knew they were expensive, but I didn't figure that," Jovan told him. "I thought you'd jump on that five hundred for an hour."

His brother gave him a look. "Nigga, is you crazy? You know how much they selling ass for in Overbrook Meadows?"

"I have no idea. I hope you don't, either."

"Sixty, seventy dollars," Luke stated. "You can get a bitch for less than that, especially if they on crack."

Jovan was disgusted. "Who the hell would want some nasty-ass crackhead? I know you not getting down like that."

"Nah, I never have."

"Well how you know how much they charge?"

"They be on Backpage," Luke told him. "You see the price right on their home page."

"What the hell is *Backpage*?" Jovan was genuinely perplexed.

"It's like Craigslist," Luke told him, "except they got *everything* on there, like escorts and stuff."

Jovan shook his head in frustration. "Yo, man, when we get home, we gotta have a serious talk."

"Cool. Save it for when we get home. For now, I'm gonna find some cheaper hoes."

"Every girl in this hotel is gonna charge the same," his brother replied. "They not stupid."

"That's *your* opinion, Jovan. You coming, or not?"

He shook his head. "Nah, man. I'ma chill."

"Alright," Luke said before he walked away. "I'll catch up with you later."

CHAPTER SIX
WHEN IN ROME...

Jovan headed for the nearest bar before he went to find Morris and Jesse. He knew his brother's extramarital activities were serious, but he never imagined Luke was hooking up with prostitutes back home.

If he was going to cheat, Jovan figured hookers were probably Luke's safest bet. Those women were not likely to get emotionally attached, so they wouldn't create a scandal or decide to kill him one day because they couldn't stand to live without him. But hooking up with prostitutes could still be a dangerous game. Jovan knew of men who followed women to hotel rooms and were ambushed by armed thugs hiding in the closet.

He thought it would be better if Luke never married in the first place, but that wasn't right. Cathy was a gem, and their children; Jovan's nieces and nephew, were wonderful. What he needed to do was convince Luke to keep his wayward penis at home, but how the hell could he do that – especially since Jovan was getting more ass than a G-string? In fact, it was probably his exploits that influenced Luke.

Ever since they were little, Luke wanted to be just like his big brother.

Jovan took a seat at the bar and ordered Cognac on the rocks. He noticed a woman sitting on the barstool next to him, but he didn't acknowledge her. He was deep in thought when the bartender served his drink.

He turned slightly and gave the woman a nod and a polite, "Good evening," before turning away.

But her smile caught his attention. He turned back to her and realized the smile was definitely focused on him.

"Hi," she said. Her eyes were sparkling.

Jovan's first thought was that he was being propositioned. If so, this woman had picked the wrong john. He never paid a woman outright for sex. He wasn't one to buy them purses or shoes, either. Lately, he didn't even take his girlfriends out to eat. They had to take him out. They bought him shoes and paid his bills.

But as he studied the woman, Jovan realized his first impression was wrong. She was a cute redhead, but her outfit and her age didn't fit the average hooker profile. She was only moderately attractive, and the crows' feet in the corner of her eyes put her age in the mid to late forties. Her dress was form-fitting, but it wasn't slutty at all. She wore pumps rather than heels, and there was no cleavage on display.

Her skin was creamy, with a few freckles on her cheeks and arms. Her crimson hair was straight, flowing past her shoulders. She had small breasts and a nice pushup bra. Her legs were long and slender, which was a turn-on. But he didn't think a middle-aged white woman was hitting on him. Then again, they were in Vegas. Maybe she went broke at the black jack table and thought she might get lucky elsewhere.

Jovan wore his dreadlocks down that night. His jeans were black, his shirt baby-blue. He had his sleeves rolled up to the elbows, exposing powerful forearms and bear-sized hands. The top three buttons of his shirt were open, and he had no tee-shirt underneath. She looked from his chest to his brown eyes and back down at his chest. Jovan wondered if this was what women with big boobs had to endure on a daily basis. Men were such jerks. But this cougar didn't have much shame, either.

"What's up?" he asked her.

She looked around before meeting his eyes. "What's your name?"

"Jovan."

She grinned at that. He wondered if she thought it was a nickname. A lot of people did.

She asked, "You wanna buy me a drink?"

Jovan continued to study her as he shook his head. "I don't buy women drinks." He would've felt bad about saying that if it wasn't the truth. He watched as her cheeks reddened.

"Okay."

He expected her to say something rude, but she didn't. He thought that was the end of their encounter when she turned towards the bartender and ordered her own cocktail. He finished his drink while the barkeep mixed hers.

She surprised him by telling the bartender, "Get him another one, whatever he's drinking."

The bartender didn't react at all, as if a white woman buying a young, black man a drink was the most natural thing in the world.

Jovan continued to watch the woman as the bartender placed the drinks before them. She had a slender face and body. He wasn't a fan of thin lips, but he liked the way she wore her makeup. Her hips had a nice spread to them. He didn't see when she sat down, but he'd guess this woman had a nice, little booty on her.

"So, what's your name?" he asked.

She said, "Sarah."

Her anxiety was obvious, and it was another clue that she was not a working girl.

"Where you from?" he asked her.

"Connecticut."

Jovan chuckled softly.

"What?" she said, smiling.

He was thinking that of course this prim and proper redhead had come from somewhere like *Connecticut*, but he didn't tell her that. There was no need to be impolite to someone who bought him a drink. Even when she built up the courage to ask him out (if that's what was happening), he'd let her down easy.

But things didn't go as planned.

"Well, how much do you charge?" she asked.

Jovan nearly choked on his drink, but he was way too cool to reveal his shock. She thought he was a prostitute. That was both scandalous and amusing. Jovan had a decent track record of using women for financial gain, but he never flat-out charged money for sex. But when in Rome...

Without missing a beat, he said, "Five hundred for an hour, a thousand for the night." He wasn't sure if those prices were acceptable, but if that's what the high-priced whores in the hotel were charging, he should be able to bring in the same.

Despite his smooth demeanor, his heart was kicking while he waited for her to respond. She studied his face a while longer and then her eyes rolled down his body. Jovan felt like a piece of meat on the butcher block.

This feeling increased tenfold when she told him, "Unbutton the rest of your shirt."

He noticed there was no please at the beginning of that statement or a question mark at the end. That meant it was an *order*, which Jovan was generally opposed to. But for a potential thousand or even five hundred bucks, he'd unbutton his shirt – and more.

He did as she requested and pulled the shirt open, so she could see his full torso. His six-pack looked a little scrunched due to his seated position, so he wasn't surprised when she asked – rather *told* him to, "Stand up."

Her voice was soft. She was very polite, but still demanding. Jovan stood and held his hands down to his sides. He thought this was one of the most bizarre encounters he'd ever experienced. Considering he was 38, there had to be another experience that was stranger than this, but for the life of him, he couldn't think of it at the moment.

A few people were watching their interaction, including the bartender. No one reacted as if something out of the norm was taking place.

Wow, Jovan mused. *This really is the city of sin.*

After examining his chest and stomach and the sexy lines under his love handles, she nodded.

"Okay. Can you meet me in room 512 – in about twenty minutes?"

He nodded. "Do you want me for an hour or...?"

She thought for a second. "Can I decide when you get up there?"

"Sure."

"Okay." Her smile was bright and perky.

She stood, and Jovan checked out her curves as she turned and walked away. Sarah had an unexpectedly plump ass. Her legs were well-toned. He might not have approached her in a crowd, but Jovan predicted he'd have a great time with her. He downed the rest of his drink and left the bar with a swagger he didn't have a few minutes ago.

Since he had twenty minutes to spare, he decided to stop by his room to freshen up. He pulled his phone from his pocket as he headed for the elevators. He planned to send his friends a text message, to let them know he may be occupied until the morning, but he ran into his brother before he got to the lobby. Luke was alone, so Jovan knew he hadn't found a cheaper prostitute yet.

"Hey, bro. Where you headed?"

"Upstairs," Jovan told him. "Gotta stop by the room before I head to *someone else's* room. I'm glad I caught you. Can you tell Morris and Jesse I might be out all night?"

"Really? What you got going on?" Luke began to walk with him.

Jovan told him about his encounter with Sarah. Luke was stunned, but not totally surprised. When it came to Jovan, picking up girls was never a problem. Women would throw etiquette to the side and approach him, even at a funeral.

"So you just ran with it?" Luke asked.

"Hell yeah. What was I supposed to do? She's offering money for sex. Who wouldn't jump on that?"

"What she look like?"

Jovan described her.

"She's a cougar?" his brother asked.

Jovan nodded. "Yeah, I guess so. I think she got ten years on me."

"You lucky motherfucker," Luke muttered. "Can I go?"

Jovan knew his jealousy was kicking in. "No. Why would you ask me that?"

"She might want *two* dudes," Luke ventured.

"If she did, she would've said so. Plus I'm not finna help you cheat on Cathy. You need to get off that shit."

"Alright, man. I was just asking. Have fun with your hoeing."

"Oh, I'm *hoeing* now?"

"You've always been hoeing," Luke told him. "But this takes it to a whole 'nother level. After tonight, you'll be a full-fledged hoe."

"Say, watch your mouth, before I dot that eye," Jovan threatened. "Don't be hating on me, just because nobody approached you."

"I'm just messing with you." Luke didn't think his brother would really hit him – not in the middle of the hotel at least – but Jovan had kicked his ass before. Some memories always stick with you.

"If she wants me all night, I'll send you a message," Jovan said as he stepped onto the elevator.

"Alright. Good luck, bro. And don't nut quick!"

Jovan laughed at that, but when the elevator doors closed he gave his brother's warning some thought. As a prostitute, or *male escort*, he would be expected to perform for as long as his client wanted. He wondered if he should rub one out before he got to Sarah's room.

He chuckled at the thought as the elevator propelled him towards his destiny.

This shit's gonna be interesting...

• • • • • •

Monica leaned with both elbows on the table, partially because Jovan wasn't speaking very loudly, but also because she was completely enthralled in his story. They'd been at the I HOP restaurant for over an hour. Their waitress had taken their empty plates, leaving only drinks on the table. It was very late in what had been a long day for Monica, but she wasn't sleepy at all. She watched Jovan's eyes and mouth as he spoke. She was not happy when he stopped.

"So," he said with a shrug, "I went up there and..." He grinned. "Things were not what I expected. There was a lot Sarah didn't tell me. But we got past it. I did my thing and got paid."

Monica almost reached across the table to throttle him.

"What do you mean *you did your thing and got paid*? How you gonna tell that whole story and breeze over the best part?" Her look of discontent was real.

Jovan chuckled. He folded his strong arms over his stomach and sat back in his seat. "I didn't think you wanted to hear the dirty details."

Monica felt like a perv for admitting she did indeed want those details, but she wasn't going to lie and say she didn't. "You said you wanted to tell me about your first client. If you're gonna tell it, tell it."

"Alright. If you wanna hear about *explicit sex*, I don't mind..."

Monica's face and chest flushed with heat. She felt like he was teasing her. "It's part of the business, right?"

"It is if you decide to manage me. Have you decided?"

"I don't know." She smirked. "Finish your story first."

Jovan sensed her decision wouldn't have anything to do with the actual story. If he didn't know any better, he'd say her reason for wanting to hear the rest of his sultry tale was gratuitous. Did his old girlfriend grow up and become a freak? He would find her a lot more interesting if that was the case. But she had a boyfriend, and he wanted her to be his manager. Those were two very good reasons not to test the waters with her.

Again he wondered why they never had sex in high school. He cursed himself for being such a wuss back then. Did he not notice Monica's hips and thighs when they were younger? Didn't he ever imagine her lips wrapped around his erection? Surely he had, or he never would've gone out with her.

"Alright," he said. "But I can't tell that story in here. We might get kicked out and banned from coming back."

"Okay. You wanna go sit in my car?"

Yup, she got a little freaky-deaky in her, Jovan decided. "That's cool," he replied. "But you gotta promise not to touch me while we're out there."

"Boy, ain't nobody trying to touch you." She scooted out of the booth and rose to her feet.

Jovan watched her ass as she walked away from the table. *Damn.* He was glad she didn't ask *him* to keep his hands to himself. He didn't like to make promises he couldn't keep.

CHAPTER SEVEN
SARAH (AND BETH)

Jovan knocked on the door of room 512 and was greeted by the woman he'd met downstairs. Sarah wore the same dress, minus her pumps. Her bare feet sank into the lush carpet of her luxury suite. Her toenails were painted red, matching her fiery mane. She didn't look nervous about the encounter, which Jovan found strange. He was certainly on edge, despite the fact that he was the powerful, possibly aggressive black guy, and she was a pretty little thing.

With a smile, she told him, "Come in."

He studied her features as he stepped inside. He decided the few crow's feet in the corner of her eyes didn't detract from her looks. She was mature and radiant. Jovan continued to admire her curves as he reached to push the door closed. He liked that Sarah was fit. He appreciated the spread of her hips, the small swells of her breasts. Despite the strangeness of their date, he thought he would enjoy making love to her. He was eager to discover if her carpet matched her drapes.

She said, "Thanks for coming," and backed into the room.

Before Jovan could reply, he was distracted by a shadow in the hallway. His immediate thought was SET UP! Had he been lured here for a robbery or arrest? He didn't recall if he'd given his brother the room number he was headed to.

His muscles tensed as his brain made quick decisions. He decided to evaluate the possible threat before choosing between fight or flight. He was relieved to see that it was another woman approaching, and she didn't have a weapon in hand. But Jovan wasn't ready to let his guard down. He looked from Sarah to the surprise guest, a frown knotting his brow.

"What the hell is this?"

"It's okay," the redhead told him.

"Hello," the new girl said at the same moment.

Sarah's friend was tall. Her hair was raven black. She wore a maroon skirt with a white blouse. Her makeup was flawless; bold eyeliner with perfectly sculpted eyebrows. Her lipstick was plum-colored. She was attractive enough to be a working girl. Jovan thought she might be around Sarah's age.

"Come," she said as she stepped into the front room. "Have a seat."

He shook his head slightly. His back was to the door, but the deadbolt wasn't engaged. Unless one of the women was an undercover ninja, he was positive he could flee the room if need be, which settled his nerves a little.

"Nah," he said. "Why don't y'all sit down and tell me what's going on. You didn't tell me somebody else was gonna be here," he scolded Sarah.

"I'm sorry," she replied. "But to be fair, you didn't ask."

She continued to smile as she took a seat on the sofa. Her friend joined her. They sat hip to hip. The brunette crossed her legs gracefully. Sarah grinned nervously, while her friend's expression remained blank. The brunette's gaze rolled down Jovan's frame before she looked him in the eyes. If she liked what she saw, he couldn't tell.

"This is Beth," Sarah said. She reached and placed a hand on her friend's thigh as she spoke.

It was a small gesture, but Jovan considered himself discerning when it came to slight nuances, especially when his subjects were women. He thought he saw something in the touch. Sarah confirmed this with her next statement.

"She's my wife."

Oh, shit. Jovan's eyebrows rose as he considered the new direction this night might take. Beth's stony demeanor made him eager to dominate her sexually. Submissive girls were rarely a turn-on. His legendary success with women kept him on constant lookout for someone who might be a challenge.

Beth immediately shut down his line of thinking. "Don't even thinking about touching me."

Jovan shook his head with an amused chuckle. He folded his massive arms over his chest and stared down at the women. He knew how intimidating his posture was.

"Alright, one of y'all need to tell me what's going on. I didn't come up here for no games."

"A *Texan*?" Beth exclaimed with a hint of sarcasm.

"I didn't ask, but I think so," Sarah responded giddily.

"She's *bi-sexual*," Beth told their guest. She said the word with clear disdain. "I don't know why she likes dicks, but I love her, and I'm willing to indulge in her desires – every now and then."

The woman spoke with the air of a CEO, someone important. Jovan could see her sitting at the head of a conference table, with well-dressed men and women seated around her.

Sarah blushed, and she took hold of her wife's hand. She pulled it into her lap and caressed it affectionately.

"Tonight my wife selected you," Beth continued. "I'll pay you to fuck her, and then you'll be on your way. I'll pay you five hundred dollars for one hour, as you and Sarah discussed."

Jovan's breathing was steady, though Beth's comments heated his chest. The warmth gradually flowed down his torso and between his legs. He had been with two women before, but never had one girl instructed him to *fuck* another. And they were married, no less. It was disappointing to know that he wouldn't be exploring any of Beth's holes (he especially wanted to slide his meat between those condescending, plum-colored lips). Nonetheless, he was willing to give the ladies what they wanted.

"Okay," he said. "Where's the money?"

He wasn't sure if getting paid up front was proper protocol, but it seemed like a good idea. It wasn't like he could take his sex back afterwards, if the women decided not to pay.

Beth gave him a look – which Jovan would describe as annoyed – before she rolled her eyes and reached into her bra. His eyes followed her thin fingers as she produced a small fold of bills from her bosom. She noticed his eyes lingering on her milky cleavage and said, "Don't look at me like that. Save your perverted eyes for her." She nodded towards her wife.

Jovan didn't think his eyes were perverted. He eyed Sarah, and she smiled agreeably. He gave her a look to mean, *Is she always like this?*

Sarah shrugged and nodded, as if she understood him perfectly.

When his attention returned to Beth, he saw that she had ten crisp one hundred dollar bills. She counted out five and placed them on the coffee table.

Jovan's eyes widened slightly. He couldn't believe this was really happening. He marveled at the ease in which this opportunity had fallen into his lap. His heart knocked as he reached for the money, but he stopped short. He looked around, wondering how many things could go wrong if he proceeded. He wasn't aware of the numerous risks people took when they accepted money for sexual favors. He was sure going to jail was only one of many pitfalls.

"Are y'all cops?"

Sarah and Beth looked at each other. The redhead giggled.

"Of course we're not," Beth said. "Do the police set up stings in *Vegas*? That would be weird."

Jovan had no idea. He knew prostitution was legal there, but he was pretty sure the working girls (and guys) had to get some kind of license.

"What about cameras?" he asked. "I don't want to be recorded." He knew he'd have no way of knowing if they'd hidden one already, but he felt like he should at least make it clear that any video produced would be against his will.

"We're not going to record you," Beth said with another flare of frustration.

"What do you mean *we*?" Jovan asked. "You're leaving, right?"

The woman looked at him as if the question was ludicrous. "I'm not leaving you alone with my wife. We're all going to the bedroom."

Jovan tried to hide his surprise as he continued to calculate and put himself in a position of advantage. "Oh, hell no. If you wanna sit there and watch, you gotta pay for that."

"Fine, sir. How much?" The brunette seemed to be struggling to keep her cool.

Jovan said, "Two hundred more."

Beth's small nostrils flared as she counted out two more bills. She placed them on the table with the rest of his money. Noticing how quickly she complied, Jovan wished he'd asked for more.

He couldn't think of anything else to inquire about, so he bent to retrieve his payment. The bills were all new. He held them up to the light, as he suspected a real prostitute would.

All of the money was legit, as far as he could tell. He stuffed it in his front pocket and said, "Alright. Let's go."

Sarah squealed with delight. She turned and kissed her wife on the cheek. Beth frowned and shied away from her, the way a husband might if he only allowed his mother-in-law to visit so his wife would shut the hell up about it.

The ladies rose from the couch and headed for the bedroom. Jovan moistened his lips as he followed them.

• • • • • •

There was a chair in the corner of the room. Beth headed for it. She took a seat and crossed her legs again. Her face remained deadpan. Sarah took a seat on the bed. Her smile was ear to ear. Jovan stepped cautiously into the room, not sure how to proceed. He looked around and didn't see anything out of the norm.

"Come here," Sarah said, reaching for him. "Take off your shirt," she breathed.

Jovan walked to her. She spread her legs, compelling him to step between them. He got a glimpse of her panties. They were black and lacy. Feeling guilty about the peek, he looked to Beth, who was no more than twenty feet away.

"Don't look at me," she said. "Look at her. She's the one who wants you."

He had to ask, "Do you have to be so rude?"

"I don't like you," Beth revealed. "You stink. You smell like a man."

Jovan frowned, not sure how to react to that.

"I like your smell," Sarah said. She grabbed hold of his shirt and pulled him closer. She began to unbutton it. *I love your smell.*"

Jovan looked to Beth again, he couldn't help it. She sneered and told him, "You better be good."

The contrasting emotions in the room were extreme. Surprisingly, Jovan was turned on by the annoyed lesbian as well as her horny wife. He shrugged out of his shirt when Sarah undid the last button. She gasped and licked her lips at the sight of his nude torso. She reached and pulled him closer. She placed her hands on his chest and moaned softly as she caressed his pectorals. Her hands were warm, her touch surprisingly soft. She ran her hands from his collarbone to his six-pack, up and down. He watched her eyes, which were filled with delight.

"You are so *fine*," she gushed. "You're *gorgeous*."

The muscles in his chest and stomach tightened as she fondled him.

She asked, "Can I kiss you – on your body?"

Jovan was surprised by the question. He wondered if it was customary in the world of prostituting. Were there hookers out there who would deny the request?

He didn't see anything out of the ordinary around her lips, so he said, "Yeah. Go for it. But don't leave any marks."

She giggled before devouring his right nipple. Her mouth was warm and enticing. He felt her tongue circle his areola as she sucked slightly. She hummed through her nostrils. Her lips skated across his chest before zeroing in on his other nipple, which she quickly brought to a state of arousal. Jovan always felt that women who slept with women had certain skills with their mouths that heterosexual women had yet to master. Sarah was no exception to the rule.

The pleasure from her soft kisses created pulses of electricity that gave him goose bumps. More waves of heat flooded his chest. He reached and clutched the back of her head instinctively but then thought better of it. He removed his hand and once again looked to Beth for assurance.

"You can touch her," the brunette said. "Grab her hair. Pull it. She likes it."

Jovan's hand disappeared in Sarah's hair again, but he didn't pull it, as instructed.

"Grab it," Beth demanded. "I told you to pull her hair."

"Okay, um, are you gonna sit there and watch *and* talk, too?" he asked.

Beth said, "If you have a problem with it, you can give me a refund now and leave."

Jovan wasn't giving the money back. That much was for certain.

"Nah, it's just, it's a little weird," he admitted.

"Do you want to leave or not?"

"No."

"Then shut up and grab her hair."

Sarah continued to lick and suck his chest the whole time, as if this conversation didn't concern her in the slightest.

He gripped her hair, hoping to punish her for the way Beth was speaking to him.

She gasped. *"Ah."*

Her mouth hung open as he pulled her head away from him. Her thin lips were swollen from kissing him. Her eyes were dreamy, almost intoxicated.

"Are you gonna suck his dick?"

Jovan realized Beth was speaking to her wife now. Her crudeness was scandalous, and it was a turn-on. Jovan's manhood grew steadily, until the bulge in his jeans was visible.

Sarah nodded eagerly. Jovan let go of her head as she scooted forward. He backed away and allowed her to slide off the bed. She went straight to her knees and reached to undo his belt. Again Jovan's eyes found Beth.

"Don't look at me!" she snapped. "I'm not sucking it. You're disgusting."

What the fuck? He wasn't sure how to respond to any of this. *Disgusting*? He didn't think a woman had ever called him that, not in the bedroom, at least. He looked down again as Sarah unbuckled his pants. He reached to pull the zipper. She slid his jeans down his legs and marveled at the bulge in his boxers.

She wrapped her hand around it and told her wife, "Oh, baby, *he's so big!*"

"I see," Beth replied. "And you wanna suck it, don't you?"

Sarah nodded as she squeezed and caressed him. "I do. I'm sorry."

Jovan didn't think she was genuinely apologetic. If so, it didn't dull her excitement.

"Here." Beth tossed a condom at them.

Sarah let go of him and scooped it up off the carpet.

"Can I take my pants off?" Jovan asked. He didn't like the idea of his jeans restraining him at the ankles. There was still a chance he might have to make a speedy getaway.

"Yes," Sarah replied. "Let me help you with your shoes."

She pulled off his loafers and assisted as he stepped out of his pants. Jovan was aware of where his money was as she set them aside. Even if there was a fire, he'd make sure to grab his pants before he ran out of there.

Sarah's eyes were glued to his erection as she pulled his boxers off. She was clearly impressed.

"*Ooh, thank you, baby.*"

Jovan thought she was speaking to him, but Beth replied, "It's not too big?"

Sarah quickly shook her head. "No. I like it big."

She gripped him again. The feel of her soft hand on his hot flesh made him pulsate in her fist.

"I can't believe you want that thing inside you," Beth said. "You're just as disgusting as he is."

"I'm sorry," Sarah replied.

Jovan noticed her trying to hide a smile as she let go of him and tore open the condom. He thought he was past the point of being surprised by anything these women said or did, but their banter made him feel like he'd walked into the Twilight Zone. Did people like this really exist; a man-hating lesbian who would purchase a prostitute for her dick-loving wife? As experienced as he was, he never would've imagined it.

He was fully erect when Sarah demurely slid the condom on. He didn't realize how badly he wanted to penetrate her until she hesitated and looked nervously at her wife. Beth shook her head, her brow furrowed.

"Well, suck it, then. What are you waiting for?"

"Nothing. I..."

The hell with this, Jovan thought. He didn't care which one, but *someone* needed to start sucking. He reached and grabbed the back of her head again.

Sarah managed to get out a surprised, "*Oh*," before he pulled her face into his lap. He pushed his hips forward at the same moment, and his meat slid deeply into her mouth. Her eyes were wide as she stared up at him, but her lips were still curved into a smile.

"Yes, shut her up," Beth said. "That's what you wanted, right, Sarah? You wanted him to shove his cock in your mouth..."

"*Mmm hmm*," the redhead hummed and tried to nod.

Jovan gripped her hair harder. He worked her head back and forth until she took over and began to do it herself. Within twenty seconds he decided she wasn't the best when it came to fellatio. But the bizarre circumstances increased his excitement tenfold.

He grabbed her head with both hands and pumped his hips deeper. Her mouth wasn't big enough to take in more than half of him, but he kept pushing, wondering how far she could go before gagging. Amazingly, she never reached that point. Even when he shoved in deeply enough to see a bulge in her throat, Sarah never complained. It was as if she had no gag-reflex. She was a champion deep-throater.

"You like that?" Beth questioned. "He's fucking your face; treating you like a whore. You like that big, black dick all the way down your throat, don't you?"

"*Um, um, umm hmmm,*" Sarah moaned around his shaft.

Jovan took that as an invitation to go deeper. He was surprised when ¾ of his dick disappeared past her lips and she still didn't complain. Due to his girth, her mouth appeared to be open to the widest point. He wondered how the hell this was possible.

She backed off for a second and began to lick his shaft. Jovan was glad for the change of pace, because he was about to cum. He didn't think it would be a problem, as long as he was able to go again. But he didn't want to reach a climax so quickly. They might realize he was some random Joe, rather than the experienced male-escort they thought they had purchased.

Beth told him, "You should cum on her face."

Jovan didn't expect that at all, given the heightened sexual awareness in the country, especially in a place like Vegas.

"You'd like that, wouldn't you?" Beth sneered. "You want him to cum in your face. You'd drink it, wouldn't you?"

"*Yes*," Sarah panted between licks.

"I know you would," Beth growled. "You're a dirty bitch."

"I am," Sarah agreed.

She gobbled him down again, and Jovan moaned with pleasure. He dug his toes in the carpet as his orgasm gained momentum. He wanted to yank the condom off and ejaculate in the redhead's face. He wanted it so badly, he could picture it as he stared down at her. He hadn't came in over a week, so it would be a good load. He imagined painting her. He could see it drizzling down her face, between her eyes.

He was foolish enough to tell them, "I'm clean." It was the truth, but Beth wasn't having it.

"You're not cumming in my wife's face, you asshole! But I should let you fuck her in the ass, just because she's such a filthy whore. You'd like that too, wouldn't you," she asked Sarah.

The redhead nodded, while maintaining suction on the dick she purchased. "*Mmm hmmm*."

"Come here," Beth snapped. "Let me take your dress off. I hope he fucks you so hard your pussy is swollen for a week. Maybe that'll teach you."

Sarah unlatched obediently and backed away from Jovan. She tried to hide her delight as she stood and approached her wife. Beth rose to her feet. Sarah turned her back to her, so she could unzip her dress. With her wife preoccupied, Sarah was free to smile wickedly at Jovan. She winked at him.

He didn't know what the signal meant, but he assumed things were going exactly as she planned. If so, he was happy to play his part. He was ecstatic, even.

• • • • • •

The rest of their hour passed quickly, much too quickly, in Jovan's opinion. Beth undressed her wife, and Sarah crawled across the bed, totally nude. Jovan approached her from behind and was pleased to find her kitty was gushing. And yes, the carpet did match the drapes.

He took her from behind while Beth continued to berate them both. Sarah may have preferred the company of women, but she was by no means a stranger to men. Jovan was able to squeeze his whole dick inside her. Her pussy was hot and welcoming. He stroked slowly at first, but that wasn't what either of his customers wanted.

"Fuck her hard!" Beth commanded. "I want to hear that ass clapping!"

Jovan did as instructed. Soon the bedroom was filled with the smacking sound of his hard thrusts. Sarah began to scream like a banshee, which was another huge turn-on for him. She buried her face in the pillows and gripped the sheets until her fingertips were white.

Jovan tried to hold it together, but as he stared down at her pink ass and watched his dick disappear between her labia, he wished he had taken his own advice and rubbed one out before coming to their room.

He was forced to tell them, "I can't go this hard without cumming."

"*She better cum first*!" Beth shrieked. "And you'd better be able to go again. We still have forty minutes."

"Alright, that's fine," Jovan panted. He tried to get his mind and his eyes off Sarah's inviting asshole. He didn't know if Beth was serious about him penetrating that opening, but he was down for it if they were.

He was grateful when the squeals in the room began to sound like someone was being murdered. Sarah's ass was fiery red from the pounding. Her thighs began to tremble as her climax rolled through her. Her walls clamped down on him and sucked him in deeper. She arched her back and hiked her ass up higher. She began to throw her hips back at the same speed of his strokes.

"Aw shit," Jovan muttered. He reached and grabbed a handful of red hair, praying he would outlast her. He yanked her head back so hard, she was nearly staring at the ceiling.

"Are you cumming?" Beth asked her. "Are you gonna cum all over that black dick?"

"*Ahh*!" Sarah screamed. "*Yes! Yes! I'm cumming!*"

Jovan pushed deeper and harder. He felt an enormous shudder roll down her whole body. He forced himself to hold it in for a little while longer as her orgasm peaked, causing her to squirm and crumble beneath him. She began to purr softly as her climax gradually zapped her strength to the point that she lay flat on her stomach.

Jovan followed her down and pumped slower, allowing her orgasm to run its full course. When her moans softened, and he was sure she was in the midst of an exquisite afterglow, he spilled his own seed.

He didn't think either of them noticed, but Beth said, "He's cumming in you now. Are you happy? This is what you wanted, right?"

"*Oh, yes,*" Sarah whispered. She closed her eyes and smiled as he pulsated inside her.

"You're disgusting," Beth said. "And you're not falling asleep on me. You're gonna get fucked some more. And you're not gonna ask me for dick again for at least four months. Do you hear me?"

"Oh, *yes*," Sarah whispered.

"You," Beth said to Jovan, "stop laying there like you're in love. You get paid by the hour, so stop wasting my time. Go wash up and come back. And you better still be hard."

Jovan was trying to enjoy his own afterglow, but the mean lady was right. This was business not pleasure. He crawled off the bed and went to wash up. He was so eager to see what other tricks the redhead had in store for him, he was still rock hard when he returned to the bedroom.

● ● ● ● ● ●

Forty minutes later Sarah lay used, abused and completely satisfied on the soiled hotel sheets. She didn't speak or open her eyes as Jovan got dressed. He thought she was asleep, but he didn't think an unconscious person could hold a smile on their face.

Beth followed him when he left the bedroom. In the front room, she asked for his phone number.

"We only come here three or four times a year," she explained. "If you're available on our next trip, Sarah would like to see you again."

She didn't seem like the same witch who had been yelling at them for the past hour.

Jovan commented, "I thought you didn't like me?"

Beth smiled. His eyes widened. He didn't think her lips ever curved that way.

"It's just a game we play," she revealed. "I don't like the idea of my wife liking dick, but I knew who she was when

I married her. *I* don't ever want to be with a man, but I won't deprive her. As far as my language, she gets more excited when I tell her how disgusting men are, and frankly, so do I. Next time, I would like to touch myself, while you screw her."

Wow, Jovan thought. This may not be the absolute freakiest couple he'd ever met, but they were certainly in the top five. He gave Beth his number. He doubted if he'd be in Vegas when they returned, but Sarah might be worth the trip, especially if he could get them to pay his airfare.

CHAPTER EIGHT
THE FINAL CHAPTER
BONAFIDE

And
As I lay
Thinking of him
His eyes, his smile
His musk, his skin
And my thighs spread
A river flows
I moan
He hears me
He comes to feel me
Taste me
Take me

Jovan chuckled as he completed his erotic story. "That's crazy, right?"

Crazy was one of the things going through Monica's head as she listened to him. But *hot* was probably at the top of her list. It wasn't just his story; she felt physically heated as well. It was mid fall. She had the front windows rolled down on her Yukon, but there was no breeze. It was 81 degrees outside but felt like 105 degrees in her car. She reached to start the engine as she held the button to make the windows rise.

Jovan said, "You hot?"

"It's not hot to you?"

He shrugged. "A little." He looked out upon the mostly empty parking lot at the I HOP.

He didn't appear self-conscious about anything he told her, but Monica felt a thin coat of sweat on her face. She was too embarrassed to wipe it off. Even the bright lights from the restaurant's marquee seemed to beam more heat their way.

"Luke says I'm a bonafide prostitute now," Jovan reported.

Monica knew his brother. Luke went to Finley High with them.

"No, not necessarily," she said, hoping to keep him from noticing how off-kilter she was. "You, you only did it one time."

"Yeah, but it's like I said…" He looked into her eyes. "I feel like my whole life has been leading up to this. Every experience I've ever had with a woman played a part in what happened at that hotel."

Monica wondered if his experiences with her were included in that comment. She doubted it, since they never made love. Plus he said "women," and she considered herself a *girl* back then.

"But why me?" she wondered. "Why'd you come to me with this?"

"I think I was meant to see you at the mixer." He was animated. His eyes were on fire. "I believe in fate. My Vegas trip was two weeks ago. Since then I've been trying to figure things out, to see if I could pull this off. I knew I was missing something, and now I realize what it is: *A manager.* You're what I need to make this work."

"It sounds like you've already been successful with it," she noted. "Why don't you just get a license in Vegas and go for it. You don't need me."

"But that's the thing. I can't move to Vegas. I got my mom here. My brother and them, they need me."

"Oh, how is your mom?" Monica asked. She hoped she didn't look surprised to hear the woman was still alive.

Jovan's mother suffered from sickle cell. She'd been defying the odds all her life. Not only did she marry and deliver two healthy boys, but she didn't pass her blood disorder down to either of them. Jovan was 38, so Monica knew his mother had to be going on sixty. It was uncommon for someone with sickle cell to live much longer than that.

"She's good," he said. "She'll be alright. You know my mama's strong."

He lost a bit of energy at that moment, which meant his prognosis was probably more hopeful than accurate. Monica didn't want to sour the mood, so she didn't ask for details.

"So you want to be a working escort in Overbrook Meadows?"

"Yeah." He nodded. "I went on that Backpage website when we got home. There are a lot of escorts on there. You can narrow it down by city, male or female. I was gonna create my own page, but I don't know how it works; how the girls avoid getting arrested for that. I mean, it seems so wide open. I'm wondering why a cop can't go on there and set up a meet. It would be an easy bust, right?"

"Yeah…" Monica thought for a second. "But they have some kind of special arrangement when it comes to payment. I don't know how they do it, but I know a few girls on there."

"No shit?"

She nodded. "Sometimes I bring strippers to the clubs I work for. They're on Backpage. Some of them are."

Jovan smiled. "So you know about it? See, that's what I'm talking about. You already got more knowledge than me. You gotta help me with this. We can start from the ground up. I think we can make a whole lotta money. I mean, I don't know if I can get a thousand a night *every night*. But if I do, you'd get fifteen percent. That's worth it, right?"

"First of all, I'd get *twenty-five percent*," she corrected him. "And what–"

"Twenty-five? That's not–"

"I charge my regular clients twenty," she informed him. "But this isn't regular, Jovan. This is illegal. I don't wanna end up going to jail for you. I got a daughter. I can't – I can't take that risk."

"Okay," he agreed. "Twenty-five. So you'll think about it?"

The money did sound tempting. Even though she was against the idea, her mind was always working; trying to figure a way to turn a dollar into twenty. She could send Jovan to a bachelorette party for five hundred bucks and charge five hundred more for every woman there who wanted to sleep with him. He was thinking small, if he didn't think he could pull in a thousand a night.

But this was a crazy idea. She shouldn't get involved.

"Tell me what you think I can do for you."

"Help me set up my Backpage account," he said. "Find out how the girls operate without getting arrested. Screen my clients and send business my way. Help me stack some money, so we can both retire. That's it."

Her eyes widened. "That's it? Jovan, that's a lot. I'm pretty sure that would make me, I don't know, your *pimp* or something."

He laughed. "Nah. A *madame*, maybe, but not a pimp."

"I'm serious."

"I am too, Monica. You know you'd be good at this. You got hookups with the clubs. You already know some escorts. Promoting is what you do. How hard would it be to find women who wanna sleep with me? I'm not saying I'm all that, but, you know…"

She thought his attempt at humility was cute. Jovan was all that, and he knew it. But this could be trouble. She was doing just fine with her current projects. She made enough to pay the bills – almost every month. She had too much on her plate. And while some of the things she currently did at work were a tad bit illegal, pimping an ex-boyfriend would take it to another level – not to mention the overall *weirdness* of it all.

"I'll think about it," she told him.

He grinned as if she'd accepted his offer. "Cool. That's a start. Here…" He pulled his wallet from his pocket and produced an old business card. "From when I was modeling," he explained as he handed it to her.

Monica took it, but she didn't think she would call. It was great seeing him again. But she thought their time together would've been better spent if they had simply hooked up for the night and continued on their separate ways. She didn't need to have the story of him, Beth and Sarah stuck in her head.

He opened the door and gave her another sweet smile before stepping out into the night.

• • • • • •

When she got home, Monica deposited her purse and keys on the kitchen counter. She felt exhausted, but her mind was racing. During the ride home she thought of all the practical reasons she shouldn't entertain Jovan or his kinky request. Once she had a nice-sized list, she considered all of the reasons she *should* get involved and only came up with one: Money.

For all she knew Jovan might blow up and become the next Magic Mike. If she got in on the ground floor, her 25% commission might actually retire her. Even if he didn't reach superstar status, she could always use a little extra money on the side. All she would have to do was point horny women in his direction. Why was that even illegal? She didn't think it should be.

She kicked her heels off in the living room. Her little piggies immediately sang a chorus of thanks. It felt great to be home. She stepped quietly on her carpeted floors. She kept the lights off, hoping not to awaken either of her sleeping beauties.

She stopped by her sister's room first. Anita was snug in her sheets, snoring softly. Monica found her daughter in the same state of slumber in the next room. She pulled the sheets up to her shoulders and gave her a kiss on the cheek. The princess didn't stir.

It was almost four a.m. when she entered her room. Monica was so weary, she could've dove into bed fully clothed. But she always felt like she needed a bath when she left the clubs. Tonight Jovan's sensual narrative made her feel extra dirty.

Ten minutes later she left the steamy shower and crawled into bed wearing a nightgown and panties. She thought about her ex-boyfriend while she bathed. He was still the only thing on her mind. She imagined how he must have looked in Vegas, when the redhead sucked his chest, and her wife rebuked them both. She couldn't get over the idea of him punishing Sarah's pussy while Beth watched and gave instruction. He said his dick was big. Monica had never seen it, but she could imagine.

She was frustrated when she couldn't fall asleep immediately. She sighed when one of her hands slipped into her panties, but she couldn't fault herself for being aroused. What woman wouldn't feel something if a man as fine as Jovan looked them in the eyes and told a story like that?

Monica stole glimpses at his lap multiple times while they sat in her car. She wondered if the story was making him hard, because it was certainly making her clit swell. But she never saw a bulge in his jeans. In retrospect, that was a good thing. She may have accidentally reached for it. Who knows what would've happened then?

She massaged her kitty, noticing how slick things were down there. She didn't think she'd be able to sleep in that condition, so she allowed her body to comfort itself. Her fingers knew her like no other. They found her bulbous clit and soothed it with slow strokes, just the right amount of friction. She considered retrieving a toy, something as big as she imagined Jovan was, but she moved them out of her nightstand last month, and she didn't want to get out of bed.

But tonight, she had something better than a sex toy. She had fresh memories – of Jovan. She saw his face behind her closed eyelids. She felt his hair falling into her face as he hovered over her. She felt his heat. She could almost feel his dick as he penetrated her, spreading her walls to the point that it hurt.

He was gentle with her, but he was demanding. He needed all of her. Monica began to squirm on the mattress as the sweet stroke of her fingers increased speed. Her pulse steadily quickened. Her mouth hung open. Her teeth glistened in the slight lamplight that penetrated her window shades.

The muscles in her thighs spasmed as her climax tore through her. Jovan was so good, she had to clamp her free hand over her mouth to keep from moaning aloud when she came. He continued to pound her box relentlessly as a flood of sensation rolled down her body, crashing into her clitoris with the force of a tsunami. She bucked her hips, and her fingers moved faster. More friction, hot and slick. She planted her heels on the mattress, lifting her body towards him as her orgasm split in two, each one just as powerful and pleasing.

She wasn't sure how long it lasted. When the electricity finally began to fade, and her ass sank back into the mattress, she felt totally depleted. Her breaths were soft but ragged. Her heartbeats were audible. Sweat glistened between her breasts. She squeezed her thighs closed over her hand and rolled slowly to her side. The tide from the tsunami receded, making her feel like she was set adrift on a small canoe. She was in a lazy river. The flow was smooth and relaxing.

Damn him.

She felt like she needed another shower.

Things would've been so much better if they had simply fucked tonight and gone their separate ways. She didn't want to have to think about Jovan again tomorrow...

KEITH THOMAS WALKER

ABOUT THE AUTHOR

Keith Thomas Walker, known as the Master of Romantic Suspense and Urban Fiction, is the author of nearly two dozen novels, including *Life After*, *The Realest Ever*, the *Brick House* series and the *Finley High* series. Keith's books transcend all genres. He has published romance, urban fiction, mystery/thriller, teen/young adult, Christian, poetry and erotica. Originally from Fort Worth, he is a graduate of Texas Wesleyan University. Keith has won or been nominated for numerous awards in the categories of "Best Male Author," "Best Romance," "Best Urban Fiction," and "Author of the Year," from several book clubs and organizations. Visit him at www.keithwalkerbooks.com.

www.ingramcontent.com/pod-product-compliance
Lightning Source LLC
Chambersburg PA
CBHW020615120726
47905CB00003B/798